Just the Right Amount of Wrath

A novel

Gary Carr

Just the Right Amount of Wrath
© 2015 by Gary Carr

All Rights Reserved

Inquiries should be addressed to:
Gary Carr
717 Ivanhoe Way
Grand Junction, CO 81506
         or
garaldcarr@hotmail.com

Cover Design by C. Mattson

Author Photo by Hutmacher

Printed in the United States of America
First Printing 2015
Library of Congress Control Number: 2015906222
ISBN: 978-1-63452-947-1

1. Fiction/Crime   2. Fiction/Suspense   3. Fiction/General

"Putting a new saddle on a dead horse won't make it go any faster."

GC

ACKNOWLEDGEMENTS

My appreciation to Tammy and Shirley for their perseverance and patience in seeing this book to completion.

PROLOGUE

The cruise started like any other. There was the hustle and bustle with luggage and paperwork. The throngs of eager vacationers were being herded into all the proper areas for processing. Some were anxious to get aboard for their first cruise. Other more seasoned travelers were patiently waiting for all the cacophony to settle down so they could get to the waiting champagne and buffet. Slowly, each passenger made their way to the front of the line to receive their sea-pass card–the plastic room key and credit card cleverly created by the cruise lines to make spending less noticeable.

As is always the case, a somewhat self-important couple arrive and delay the process because they think rules are for other people. Over and over the clerk states that they must have a passport or they won't be allowed to sail. Never mind the fact that they were sent at least twenty notices and reminders with every communication from the cruise line. When it finally dawns on them that their belligerent and degrading responses to the clerk won't get them aboard, they finally step aside and let others get on with checking in.

It was then that a customer service agent politely approached them and assisted them in contacting friends back home to have copies of their passports faxed to them so they could get aboard. Shortly thereafter, the couple, with a much more humble and polite attitude, boarded the ship telling everyone and anyone who would listen about their ordeal. A few short hours later, most of the passengers were settled into the buffet area to begin a food binge that would last the entire cruise.

It wasn't until later that night, after the ship had already pulled away from the dock and was entering international waters, that the body was found. The luggage handlers had delivered all of the Volkswagen-sized suitcases to the staterooms and were cleaning up the luggage area when they noticed there was still one suitcase that had not been delivered.

There were no identifying tags or cabin number as to where to deliver the case, so the crew called security as a precaution.

They had been trained to note possible terrorist threats and weren't taking any chances by moving the suitcase.

A diminutive Indonesian security officer was on the scene right away. He examined the case from all sides and ran an explosive test swab over the outside. Getting no beeps from his machine, he decided to move the case to one side so the crew could finish up their cleaning duties. To the crew, this was just another inconvenience making their day even longer. When the security officer tried to lift the heavy suitcase, it fell over, burst open and an arm fell out. Startled, the security officer jumped back and called his supervisor. The supervisor appeared, trailing a contingent of security officers and one of the ship's photographers.

The suitcase was moved to an area where it could be isolated from the confusion in the hold. When the supervisor opened the case fully, he found the naked body of a woman. He guessed the woman to be in her twenties or early thirties. She had dyed-blond hair, blue eyes, and a small butterfly tattoo near her shoulder just above her left breast. The officer donned latex gloves and carefully removed the body. He placed her on a tarp near the case and covered her with a blanket.

By this time, the ship's doctor and the staff captain had arrived. The doctor began a methodical inspection of the body. The staff captain called over the crewman who found the body and had him tell what happened. According to the crewman, the suitcase was in the middle of the luggage cage. This particular cage had been loaded early in the afternoon and was among the first being unloaded. The staff captain noted the crewman's name and ID tag number. He thanked him and released him to return to work. Based on the crewman's information, he concluded the suitcase was placed on the dock late morning as new passengers were arriving and those on the ship were disembarking. The staff captain made a note to talk with all the people involved with luggage, but didn't think it would garner anything. Whoever did this knew this was the most confusing and hectic part of a cruise ship coming into port, restocking and preparing to leave again.

The doctor, meanwhile, determined that there were no gunshot wounds, stab marks or signs of blunt force trauma. Moving along the face, he saw signs of petechial hemorrhage and discoloration from ligature marks on the throat. He also noted that the marks were probably from a garrote, something he hadn't seen since a brief internship at the county morgue. Unless other indicators appeared in an autopsy, the initial cause of death was most likely from strangulation. The doctor had the photographer take numerous photos and he recorded copious notes on his small digital recorder. He estimated time of death to be at least twenty-four to thirty-six hours ago. This meant the woman was most likely strangled the night before and brought to the pier this morning.

There was no identification on the body or in the case. An old tag in one of the suitcase pockets had a Goodwill Industries price tag for ten dollars, but nothing to indicate which store it may have come from. This seemed unusual because this was a very expensive piece of luggage. Perhaps the tag was from something inside the suitcase. The doctor placed the tag in a plastic bag, then had one of the crewmen wrap the case in a large plastic bag and tape it shut to preserve any evidence. He then had a gurney brought in, and with help, loaded the body on the cart. He motioned to the staff captain and together they escorted the woman's body to the medical center.

"Well, Dr. Bramley, any thoughts?" asked the staff captain, Paolus Popindreau.

"Whoever did this is probably not an amateur."

"Why do you say that?"

"Those ligature marks on the neck fit the pattern of a garrote. They're even all around the neck. Not like if someone used their hands. Whatever was used circled the neck and applied pressure equally on all sides. It nearly ruptured the skin as well. That's something you only get from a garrote. The fact that it was a large diameter rope or something is the only reason she didn't have a severely cut throat."

"Sure looks like a professional job to me, too. Someone went to a lot of trouble to slow identification down. They also had to know something about a ship's timing and loading process. Somehow, they were able to slip her body on board without being noticed by our security."

"I thought that a little odd myself. Aren't we supposed to x-ray and scan each bag for explosives? How do you not detect a body?"

"You don't. I'm going to have to find out if the case was even checked and how it got past security. I need to get up to the bridge and report to Captain Stephalos."

"Good idea. Let me know what happens next. This whole mess could start to get complicated."

"I'll have Ernesto set up an area in one of the refrigerated holds to store the body and suitcase once you have completed your exam."

"Excellent. That will free up the medical center and Ernesto can secure everything a lot better. Tell him he can pick up our Jane Doe in an hour. I need to take fingerprints, blood samples and facial photos so we can find out who she is."

"Fine. I'll have Ernesto check with you in an hour."

ONE

Harry Walters was sitting in his office in San Diego contemplating all the ramifications of his recent visit to Santa Barbara. He was still not sure he understood all that had happened.

First, his former partner, Tommy Thompson, had been shot and killed by his wife, Sandy, who also tried to kill Harry's ex-wife, Dayna. Then Harry was shot by a jealous dentist who had dated Dayna. All of that was wrapped up in a huge drug and money-laundering operation that Tommy Thompson set up, headed up by Rudolfo Arona in Tijuana. Harry was pleased that they had been able to get Sandy convicted and that he and Dayna were now back on speaking terms. He was still bothered, however, by the fact that the money–millions of dollars–had never been found.

Before Santa Barbara, Harry was involved in a murder trial and drug mess in Hawaii. Harry had flown to Molokai to spend some quiet time at his vacation home. His solitude was interrupted when he agreed to defend a teenage girl who had been charged with her father's murder. Harry reflected on the case and was pleased that the girl was innocent.

He also had formed a close bond with the investigative team he hired in Hawaii. He chuckled to himself as he recalled the somewhat diverse crew he had formed.

There was Melvin Momi, a Japanese-Hawaiian, who is a former Army CID agent with a private detective agency on the island of Oahu; his main side kick, Tyler Wilson, a Tongan, and one of the largest men on the planet; Patty Alemo, Harry's part-time secretary on Molokai, who is a walking compendium of knowledge about everything and everyone on Molokai; Honey Boy Vili, a large Samoan, a detective working for Melvin and also Patty's boyfriend; and, last but not least, Mei Li, also known as "The Chinaman," a supposed assassin who had been working for a drug lord and joined the team after Melvin convinced her she was on the wrong side. Harry laughed out loud thinking about tiny Mei Li and giant Tyler getting married. Harry guessed that "opposites do attract."

After Harry was shot in Santa Barbara, he had Melvin and Tyler fly from Hawaii to work with Forest Markham, his investigator from San Diego.

Harry glanced down at a piece of his letterhead and read, "Harold Walters, Attorney at Law Specializing in Criminal Defense." He thought to himself, if I'm such a damn specialist, how did I get myself into that mess in Santa Barbara? Worse yet, I still haven't taken the extended vacation I planned when I headed off to Hawaii. Maybe I'll go down to my condo in Acapulco and see if I can relax there.

Just as Harry returned to reality and resumed his review of pending cases, his secretary, Sunny Norton, knocked lightly on his office door. "Come in," Harry entreated, and she walked directly to the front of his desk. A bit surprised by this unusual behavior, Harry looked at her serious face and asked, "What's up?"

"A man just walked into the office and said he needs to talk to you about a very urgent matter."

"What's his name?"

"That's just it. He wouldn't give me his name or tell me anything else. When I told him I would call security if he didn't identify himself, he said, 'Tell Mr. Walters it's about Santa Barbara.'"

"Does he look like a dentist?"

Sunny stared back at him incredulously and said, "No. Actually he is a very good-looking Hispanic gentleman with good manners and a beautiful smile."

"Let him in and call security. I'd like them close by if we should need them."

Sunny walked back, opened the door, and motioned for the man to enter. He walked in quickly and closed the door. Startled to see the man he recognized as Rudolfo Arona in his office, Harry asked, "What are you doing here?"

In perfect English, not the heavy Spanish he used in Tijuana, Arona said, "Mr. Walters, I need your help. I'm going to be arrested for murdering my wife."

Still rattled by Arona's presence, and even more by what he said, Harry asked, "Why are you coming to me? You're one of the last people I expected to see after all that happened in Santa Barbara."

"May I sit?"

"Of course, Mr. Arona, pardon my manners."

"It's because of all that happened in Santa Barbara, and your involvement, that I want your help." He reached into his jacket and withdrew a two-fold wallet that he opened to reveal his photograph, Drug Enforcement Agency credentials and a federal law enforcement badge.

"I couldn't tell you who I really was while you were in Santa Barbara. I was still undercover in Mexico trying to ferret out the kingpin in charge of the money-laundering and the drug cartel operation. I spent three years working my way up to the middleman position in Tijuana. I was close to learning where all the money was when Mrs. Thompson shot her husband and threw everything into a tail spin."

"We can get into all this history later. First, I want to know exactly why you said you're going to be arrested for murdering your wife."

"Last week I began to notice a change in how Estaban and Ramon…you remember them?"

"Yes. They're the two watchdogs you sent to Santa Barbara to keep an eye on us."

"Right. Anyway, Estaban and Ramon began to treat me with a little less respect and I was never left alone. One or the other was always near me. Then I noticed they were taking turns staking me out at home. This went on for a couple of days and I began to fear for my wife. I told her to pack some clothes and come up here to San Diego to stay with her mother. I haven't heard from her since."

"I still don't understand. Why do you think you'll be arrested?"

"One of the cartel's favorite tactics is to use secondary targets as leverage to keep their underlings from talking and drawing attention directly to the group. I know several people who were framed for the murder of a relative killed by the cartel."

"Has your wife been killed?"

"I don't know for certain. I'm praying against all odds that there is some other reason I can't get in touch with her, but I sincerely doubt it."

"So, does the DEA know what's going on?"

"No. My supervisor and the regional director both know I'm working undercover, but I don't think they know I went into Mexico. They wouldn't have authorized my leaving the United States. As far as they know, I'm in the Santa Barbara area. That's why I kept everything so low-profile there, and why I had Sharon deliver my reports. There's no way Sharon would have told them

I was actually in Tijuana.

"So why did you come to me? Doesn't the agency have legal counsel you can use?"

"You're one of the best attorneys in California, according to everyone I talked to. Besides, I saw first-hand what you and your team are capable of doing. I want you and your investigators to find out what happened to my wife as quickly as possible, just in case she may still be alive. We can worry about my being arrested when the time comes."

"What about your safety? Do you have a safe place to stay?"

"Safe enough. I'm not worried about me. I've worked undercover for almost ten years. I know how to become invisible when I need to."

"Sounds like Tyler."

"Tyler?"

"Sorry. He's the big Tongan fellow I had as a bodyguard at the Santa Barbara Hospital."

"Just one more reason I'd rather use you than the agency."

"Okay. I'll see what I can do to help you, but I need to talk with your supervisor at the DEA. They sometimes get a little testy about outside intervention."

Arona handed a business card across the desk. "Here's the name and contact information."

"I'm going to need some time to pull everyone together. Do you have a secure phone I can call if I need to talk with you?"

Arona scribbled the number on a piece of paper from Harry's desk, then handed him a manila envelope.

"What's this?"

"Photos and detailed information on my wife, and my agency dossier. By the way, my real name is Kevin Whitehill. My wife's name is Sharon. Sharon's mother is a sweet little lady who is rather fragile health wise. I don't want to alarm her, or tip off anyone who may be watching her, that I'm worried."

TWO

"Bart Symington, you old dog, how's life treating you?"

"Bramley? Is that you?"

"Sure is. And I have a job for you."

"A job? Are you still playing doctor on cruise ships? It's been awhile."

"I am. And for the record, I'm a better doctor than you."

"Okay. Okay. Let's not start that all over. What do you mean you have a job for me?"

"We found a dead woman in the luggage bay. We don't have an ID yet and I haven't started an autopsy, but it looks like she was garroted and dumped into a suitcase. I was wondering if you could help me with the forensics on this."

"Are you in port?"

"No. We are headed to Hawaii. Otherwise I would have turned her over to the San Diego medical examiner."

"So how am I supposed to help you when you're out in the middle of the Pacific?"

"I'll talk with the captain and see if he can arrange a chopper to fly you out. We're only a couple hundred miles away. If not, I'll have the computer boys hook us up with sound and cameras for the autopsy."

Why not just come back to port?"

"Do you have any idea how much even a one-day delay costs a cruise ship? Let alone all the negative publicity. From all indications, she's not even a passenger. I think someone dumped her on purpose. I just don't know why they would pick a cruise ship. They had to know the body would be found eventually."

"I'll be glad to help, Jim. Let me know what the captain says."

"Thanks. I'll get back to you as soon as I can."

Buoyed up by Symington's willingness to help, Dr. Bramley called the staff captain, Paolus Popindreau, and told him that he had contacted Symington. He gave him a brief background of Symington's forensic expertise and asked to have him flown aboard to do the autopsy.

"I'm not sure I can talk Captain

Stephalos into flying him out. Can't he oversee the autopsy by satellite?"

"Of course. But he's a very well-respected forensic pathologist, and it'll serve us better from a public relations standpoint to have him on board personally conducting the autopsy. Since he's doing this as a friend, the only cost will be the chopper. Having him do all the police paperwork is worth the expense. Does the cruise director have anyone he can fly in or out for the entertainment venue to make the flight more cost effective?"

"I almost forgot about the police. Perhaps we should have them send an officer out with the doctor. We could take a supporting role. I'm sure Captain Stephalos wouldn't mind, and corporate probably wouldn't care if we distanced ourselves from this as far as possible."

"Great. Just give me the word and I'll call Symington."

———

Bramley thought for a moment or two about all he needed to do, then dialed Ernesto Lopez, the security officer.

"Ernie, Dr. Bramley. Can you come

to the medical center and give me a hand figuring out exactly what we're going to do with this body?"

"Be right there. I just have to go over our safety protocols with a couple of new staff members. I'll see you in about ten minutes."

Bramley liked Ernesto. He was a real pro at his job. It was easy to see why the cruise line hired him. He was always smiling and friendly to passengers and staff, while still being very efficient at keeping everyone within the lines. Ernesto was a former Army CID officer in Hawaii and hired on with the cruise ship to see the world.

––––––––––––

When Bramley uncovered the woman's body, he noticed bruise marks on the wrists and upper arms that he had not seen initially. He took several digital photos and made notations on his clipboard. As he was examining the face, Ernesto came in. "Find anything useful, Doc?"

"I don't know how useful it is, but it appears her hands and upper arms were tied before she was strangled."

"What about her feet?"

"I haven't checked yet. Let's take a look." Uncovering the body fully, both stared down at large bruises on the ankles.

"That confirms it, Doc. She was definitely tied up. There certainly isn't any doubt that this was a murder. Any word from Popindreau on what we do next?"

"Not yet. I suggested they fly a detective and pathologist over from San Diego and let them take over."

"Not interested in getting bogged down in a big murder case, huh?"

"Ernie, I'm on a cruise ship for the same reason you are: easy duty. I've been there and done that, as the saying goes. Beyond the curiosity of finding out who she is, I'm really not interested in hours and hours of examination and paperwork."

"Good point. But I still have that spark in me that wants to see justice done. No one deserves to die like this, especially a beautiful young woman."

Just then, Popindreau walked in and told Bramley and Ernesto, "Captain Stephalos got the okay from corporate to fly in your pathologist friend. The San Diego Police Department said they were familiar with Dr. Symington's work and didn't feel it necessary to send a detective, especially if you and

Ernesto concur with his findings. They suggested shipping the body back to San Diego when we reach port in Honolulu. In the meantime, they'd like photos, fingerprints and fluid samples sent back on the copter so they can begin work on their end to identify the body."

"I'll call Dr. Symington now while you're here so you'll be aware of the details and time frame."

"I still need everything in writing for the captain, but nice attempt at avoiding the paperwork."

"Win-a-few, lose-a-few."

"Bart, this is Jim again. Pack your bags. You just won an all-expense-paid cruise."

"So you got approval? That was fast."

"Even the San Diego Police are comfortable letting you do everything without a detective looking over your shoulder."

"Well, I have done a lot of work for and against them. Haven't had any of my findings refuted yet."

"How soon can you be ready? The captain says he can have a charter helicopter ready within the hour."

"Whoa. I'm going to need a couple of hours to rearrange schedules and find people to cover for me. How about we shoot for two o'clock this afternoon? That will give me three and a half hours."

"You do what's necessary. I'll call you back in an hour or so and let you know when a car can pick you up."

"Do I just get to sail to Hawaii, or do I get to do the whole cruise?"

"The whole cruise if you have time. I'll even have some good Chardonnay chilling and waiting for you."

"Set me up in a nice suite and I won't even bill you for my time."

Bramley glanced at Popindreau who was listening to the conversation on the speaker phone. He nodded approval.

"Done. I'll call you back after eleven o'clock."

THREE

Symington was excited to hear he was going to Hawaii again. He hadn't been there since he flew over to help his friend, Harry Walters, with forensics on a murder case.

Walters was a criminal defense attorney whom he had worked for on a number of occasions. They became close friends over the years. He liked Walters. He was a straight-shooter, and was more interested in justice than winning cases. He was also a fellow oenophile who was very fond of Prosecco, whereas Symington preferred his heavily-oaked Chardonnay. Thinking of Walters, he picked up his cell phone and called him.

"Good morning. Why am I so lucky to be the recipient of a Dr. Symington phone call?"

"Wanted to share some good news, Harry. I'm headed to Hawaii!"

"Dr. Wong needs your help again on

Molokai?"

"No. I'm being flown out to a cruise ship to do an autopsy on a body they found in the luggage bay."

"That's different. Was it one of the passengers?"

"No. They're all accounted for. Evidently, someone killed a young woman, stuffed her body in a suitcase, and then dumped it at the pier where the cruise ship picked it up along with all the other luggage."

"That's certainly out of the ordinary. Looks like you'll be enjoying another mystery."

"I know. And I get a free trip to Hawaii!"

"Keep in touch. I'd like to hear how it all turns out."

"Will do."

Symington was waiting for the livery service to pick him up. Bramley had told him he was booked on a corporate helicopter charter. The dark executive sedan pulled into the parking lot and stopped in front of him. The uniformed driver deftly stepped out of the car and inquired, "Dr. Symington?"

Symington nodded and the driver motioned for him to step to the rear door. He waited until he was inside and comfortably seated before loading his luggage.

"Dr. Symington, I've been instructed to take you to Montgomery Field just off the Cabrillo Freeway. Is that correct, sir?"

"Yes. Thank you."

When the executive car arrived at the helicopter facility, Dr. Symington was met by the pilot who helped the driver load his luggage on the chopper.

"This should be a short flight, Doctor. The last position I had on the cruise ship was about 160 nautical miles out, averaging seventeen knots." Patting the sleek Eurocopter Astar 350 helicopter lovingly, he added, "This little baby can get us there in an hour and a half. Your patient won't have long to wait."

"No hurry, son. I'm a forensic pathologist. The patient no longer needs medical attention, just an autopsy to determine cause of death."

FOUR

After Arona/Whitehill left, Sunny entered Harry's office and asked, "What was that all about and who is our mystery guest?"

"That was Kevin Whitehill. He was one of the key players in that mess up in Santa Barbara."

"I don't recall anyone by that name being involved in that case."

"Perhaps you remember him as Rudolfo Arona from Tijuana."

"That was Arona?" Sunny moved to a chair and placed her elbows on Harry's desk. Cupping her chin, she looked at him expectantly and said, "Now I really am curious. Can you tell me about it?"

Harry pondered whether there was any reason why he couldn't or shouldn't share Arona's conversation with Sunny. She is one of the few people he actually trusts. Erring on the side of caution, Harry merely told her that Arona was really an undercover

DEA agent and had some inside information about what was going on in Santa Barbara.

"That's it? Can't tell me any more, huh?" Looking a bit disappointed, she walked out of the office.

"I'll fill you in more when the time comes," Harry said as she neared the door.

"I know. I know. But it would sure be nice to see him again."

"Sunny Norton!" Harry exclaimed. "You're a married woman."

"That doesn't mean a girl can't enjoy a little eye candy now and then."

"I suppose you're right. Can you get ADA Williams on the line for me? I'd like to discuss a couple of legal matters with him."

When Sunny left his office, Harry pulled out a yellow legal pad and jotted down the salient facts about his conversation with Arona. After reading what he wrote, he formed a lot of questions about what Arona had told him. It must have been the surprise of him just walking into the office that kept Harry from asking things like when and where did he last see his wife? Has he or his wife talked with the DEA? And most im-portantly, how does he know something is wrong? Harry mused that taking his story about being set up at face value could be a big mistake for Arona as well as for himself.

———————

The intercom rang and Sunny announced that ADA Williams was on the line.

"Good afternoon, Ray. How's everything at the courthouse?"

"Just fine, Harry. I got a guilty verdict on that drug dealer from Chula Vista. Even you couldn't have gotten him off."

"I know. That's why I sent him down the ladder to one of the young pups for a little experience. How did Davidson do?"

"Admirably. You trained him well, Harry. All he needs is a little more courtroom time. Is that what you wanted to talk to me about?"

"That was part of it. I also want to know if you have any trustworthy contacts with the DEA in this region."

"That sounds like the tip of an iceberg. Why do you want to know?"

"I may have to represent one of their undercover agents in a criminal matter. I need to find out how well he's liked and supported. As you know, they occasionally hang underlings out to dry if they stray too far outside the lines."

"Still bitter about that kid a couple of years back? The one who decided to fund his own retirement account with agency money?"

"Damn right. They were all for his plan until the press found out and accused his supervisors of complicity. I don't want to run into that same problem again."

"Is this someone I may be prosecuting?"

"Most likely. But I'm going to do all I can to see that he never gets to court. Don't worry. If this is as complicated as I think, we'll have to work together to get to the bottom of it. This 'possible' client may be a very small part of the iceberg."

"Okay, Harry. I'll tell you who I deal with at the DEA, but the minute you have an actual client you're on your own."

"Fair enough. Who can I talk to?"

"Her name is Brenda Carlson. She's a division supervisor in the San Diego office. And just a hint Harry: she's the straightest arrow agent I've ever dealt with. You break one of the rules with her and she'll cut you off at the knees."

"Tough old biddy, huh?"

"Tough, yes. But not old or biddy, unless you cross her. Come to think of it, she looks a lot like your ex-wife."

"Oh great. Just what I need."

"Good luck, Harry. Let me know when we're not talking again."

"You got it. Thanks."

FIVE

Forest Markham was sitting in the shade of his boat's canopy enjoying a chilled IPA when he heard his radio squawking. "Angel of Mercy, this is San Diego base. Do you copy? I repeat. This is San Diego base. Angel of Mercy, do you copy?"

Markham slowly rose and ambled to the cabin. Picking up the radio handset, he pushed the talk button and answered, "This is Angel of Mercy. Come in San Diego base."

"Sorry to bother you, old man, but your legal friend has been trying to reach you by satellite phone."

"I shut the nuisance off. Did he say why he needs to talk with me?"

"All he said to tell you is, 'Arona came to see me and it's urgent!'"

"Thanks. I'll call him right away. Angel of Mercy out."

As the radio returned to its normal crackling and hissing, Markham went below and dug around through a pile of dirty clothes on his bed until he found his phone. He checked to make sure the base was up and running, then turned the phone on and tapped in the number for Harry's office. While he was waiting for someone to answer, he slid comfortably back into his spot in the shade and took another drink of beer.

"Harold Walters' law office. May I help you?"

"You certainly may, Mrs. Norton. You can start by jettisoning that ugly chap you're married to and joining me on the Angel of Mercy. We can see the world together."

In a much colder and more formal tone, Sunny responded, "Mr. Walters has been trying to reach you, Mr. Markham. If you will hold for a moment, I'll connect you."

"That would be most kind of you, Mrs. Norton," Markham responded in kind, chuckling to himself.

"Harry, Forest Markham is on the phone. And would you please tell that old goat to quit hitting on me?"

"Certainly. Ring him through."

"Markham, where are you now? I've got some interesting news. But, first, my secretary has asked that I tell 'that old goat' to stop hitting on her. You're not really hitting on her, are you?"

"No. Just some light reverie from an old English sea dog. I'm flattered she thinks so! I'm just off-shore from Catalina Island doing a bit of spear fishing and a lot of beer drinking. What's the news?"

"Rudolfo Arona walked into my office yesterday. He asked if I would help him because he's going to be arrested for killing his wife."

"Arona killed his wife and wants you to defend him? That man has some cojones!"

"Yes, he does, but the entire story is even stranger. He's not Arona. His name is Kevin Whitehill, and he's a DEA agent working undercover in Tijuana."

"That's a little dicey, considering everything we know about his activities and what he was in charge of in Santa Barbara. So how and when did he kill his wife? And why come to you to defend him?"

"That's just it. He says he didn't kill her. He thinks the Mexican cartel is setting him up. As far as I know at the moment, she's only missing. He's gone into hiding somewhere here in San Diego."

"Man, I've got to quit drinking this beer. None of what you just told me makes any sense." Markham tipped the bottle and emptied its contents into the ocean, then stowed the empty in a recycling tub at the rear of the boat. He approached the controls and started up the Angel of Mercy as he continued listening to Harry relate Arona's story.

"Was that your engine I heard?"

"Right on. I'll be able to get to San Padre tonight and catch a commuter flight to San Diego in the morning. I presume you called because you need someone to check this whole story out?"

"Right, as usual. I need to verify that Arona is really DEA agent Kevin Whitehill and has a wife named Sharon. Then I need you to start a quick search for said Mrs. Whitehill. Let me know your schedule and I'll have Sunny pick you up at the airport."

"She won't like that."

"Don't worry about Sunny. If she was really concerned about you, she would be the first to let you know."

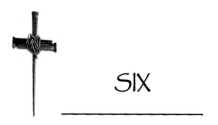

SIX

Arona was sitting at a small table in his safe house near Old Town in San Diego. He had leased the house before ever taking the assignment to infiltrate Tijuana. It was a pleasant two-bedroom affair in a nice neighborhood. It had good access to the freeway, airport and waterfront and was screened from neighboring properties by shrubs and trees. He had told the landlord he needed the house for a client who came into San Diego and wanted a homey place to stay out of the hustle-and-bustle of downtown. Since he had paid a sizeable damage deposit in cash and arranged with a local property management company to take care of the house and any maintenance, the landlord considered him his best renter.

"How in the hell did they find out?" Arona asked out loud. "I haven't had any contact with the DEA since they made me jefe in Tijuana. I'm sure Estaban and Ramon aren't smart enough to catch on. They aren't even bright enough to hide the fact that they know something. That only leaves several possibilities. Someone in the agency, my wife, someone in the Mexican system, someone I busted that recognized me, or just a screw-up on my part."

Now he was thinking, pacing, working on the possibilities. Sharon would never blow my cover. She was working undercover vice for the LAPD when we met. She knows all the rules, and besides that, I made sure not to give her any details on this assignment. A move that was for her protection as well as mine. She can't tell anyone anything she doesn't know.

He paused in his mental analysis for a moment; he let his thoughts concentrate on his wife and how they met. The more he thought of her, the deeper a sense of foreboding enveloped him. He said a soft prayer out loud, pleading with God for her safety, then returned to his analysis.

There is no way to determine if someone recognized me as a cop. So that just leaves a leak in the agency or a Mexican official who is dirty. After several minutes of thought about the DEA, he concluded it highly unlikely anyone had turned on him.

Most of the people he worked with were experienced agents like himself who had also worked undercover. They were all dedicated to good law enforcement.

That left the Mexicans, and opened a Pandora's Box of possibilities. The boss he worked for in Tijuana was someone he had never met. He didn't know his name or anything about him. He always dealt with him on the phone. For all he knew, his boss could be an undercover Mexican Federale who thought Arona was working both sides of the fence. Or better still, maybe he was dirty and felt Arona was getting too close.

"This is nuts," he blurted aloud. "I've got to quit all this thinking and just find Sharon." Changing his mental process to the task at hand, he listed all of his contacts, then methodically began prioritizing his to-do list to find her.

As reluctant as he was to contact Sharon's mother, he called her first, hoping an out-of-the-blue call wouldn't worry her.

"Hi, Edith. This is Kevin. How are you?" After patiently waiting for the conclusion of a detailed medical report on all of Edith's real and imagined maladies, he said, "Glad to hear you're doing a little better. Say, Sharon wouldn't happen to be there, would she?"

Edith immediately became alarmed. "No. Was she supposed to be here? Something hasn't happened to her, has it?"

"No. No. No. Nothing's happened. I've just been out of town for a couple of days and she wasn't here when I got home. I tried calling, but her cell phone was off. You know her. She always turns her phone off when she's driving. I just thought she might be headed your way or was out shopping, so I decided to give you a call. If she shows up, would you have her call me?"

"Of course. You know I worry about you two. Always gallivanting around all over the place. When are you going to settle down and start giving me grandchildren?"

"Edith, Edith, Edith. Take care of yourself. I'll talk with you later."

Tears welled up in his eyes. He thought about them having children and one day becoming a real family. He shook his head to clear those thoughts. Back to the to-do list. The first thing he had to do was find her.

Kevin knew all of the regular search options were not available to him. Any attempt at checking hospital admissions, filing a missing persons report, contacting co-

workers or mutual friends or using agency re-
sources would only point to some involvement by him. On the other hand, no effort on
a husband's behalf to find his missing wife
could be considered as his trying to hide
something.

There had been no contact from law
enforcement saying Sharon was incarcerated,
nor contact saying her body had been found.
There had been no calls at all to his "home"
cell phone. If his worst suspicions were true,
that the cartel had killed her to teach him a
lesson, why hadn't she been found? That left
the possibilities of the cartel kidnapping her,
or something happening to her outside the
scope of his work.

SEVEN

As the helicopter approached the cruise ship, Symington watched the crew scurrying to make sure the helipad area was cleared and all passengers moved back a safe distance. Several hundred passengers, all with cameras and cell phones in hand, lined the deck railing and watched as the chopper softly touched down. A tall, distinguished gentleman stepped out carrying a medical bag. The pilot helped unload Symington's luggage. As Symington moved to the edge of the helipad, the pilot lifted off and headed back to San Diego.

Greeting Symington were Dr. Bramley and Mr. Lopez, who ushered him to a nearby suite. Once inside, Bramley inquired, "How was the trip?"

"Short. That Astar 350 is a great ride--fast and quiet. Thank whomever you need to for shelling out the extra dough for the service."

"Is the suite satisfactory?" Bramley asked with a bit of a smug smile on his face. Bramley had arranged an owner's suite for Symington and knew he would appreciate all the finery.

'Wow! This is more than I expected. How much of a problem is this body going to be for you guys?"

"A bit. But having you here to take all the flack is worth it, right, Ernesto?"

"Glad to have you aboard, Dr. Symington. An old friend of mine in Hawaii said you're one of the best at what you do. His word is good enough for me."

"Who might that be? Anyone I know?"

"Perhaps. He said he worked with you on a murder case on the island of Molokai. His name is Melvin Momi. He's a private detective on Oahu."

"Melvin? Sure! Great fellow. It was my pleasure to work with him."

"We were Army CID together. He taught me all I know."

"Then you must be very good at your job. I'd be interested in your insight as we go along. How soon do you want me to get started?"

Bramley answered, "Will an hour

give you enough time to unpack and settle in?"

"That would be fine."

"The medical center is on deck two amidships. Can you find your way or should we send someone to guide you?"

"I'm sure I can find it. See you in an hour."

Symington glanced around the stateroom and liked all he saw. He walked over to the bar area and was delighted to see several bottles of his favorite Chardonnay in the refrigerator. There was also a small tray of appetizers that he removed and began to nibble on as he unpacked.

———

Finding the medical center was no problem. As he walked in, he was greeted by a very attractive attendant who asked if she could help him.

"I'm Dr. Symington. I'm here to see Dr. Bramley.

"He's expecting you. Right this way, please, and welcome on board."

"Thank you….Miss?"

"Klemenic. I'm from Romania," she proudly announced in the company spiel.

Entering into a large area used as a combination examining/surgery room, Symington greeted Bramley, "I found my way without any help. Let's get started."

Bramley and Lopez had the woman's body covered with a white sheet on a large stainless steel table. Bramley walked over to the table, removed the sheet and said, "She's all yours. Let me know how I can help."

"Do you have a recorder?"

"Here you go," said Bramley handing him a palm-sized digital recorder.

"Next, I would like a headlight and a loupe if you have one."

Bramley supplied him with the required items and watched as Symington donned a smock and gloves, then began an extensive examination of the body.

Turning the recorder on, Symington started with his usual prefacing remarks, noting the location of the autopsy, the date and time of commencement, and the names of those in attendance. Continuing, he said, "This is Dr. Bart Symington. I am examining the body of a woman who appears to be between twenty-five and thirty years of age, five feet, two inches tall and approximately one hundred ten pounds."

He went on for another half hour,

reaffirming what Dr. Bramley had first noted when he found the body.

"Looks like someone spent some time torturing this young lady before killing her."

"How did you come to that conclusion?"

"Mostly by the bruising on her upper arms and stomach. It looks like someone held her very tightly by the arms while someone else punched her repeatedly in the stomach and ribs. I think we'll find extensive internal bruising and bleeding when we open her up. Whoever held her had large hands. You can see imprints on her biceps." Placing his hand next to the marks, he said "See, the hand is bigger than mine and I have pretty large hands."

"So they held her, beat her, and then killed her. I wonder if they were trying to get information out of her."

"That's what I think. There doesn't seem to be any sexual assault and her death appears to be by strangulation. Add all that together, and I'd say you have a very obvious case of homicide."

"I knew that when we first found her."

"Jim, don't get touchy. I'm just confirming your findings. I agree that something like a garrote was used to strangle her because of the dimension and consistency of the bruises on her neck. I'll be very surprised if anything else shows up."

Symington retrieved his bag, opened it, and began removing a collection of scalpels and other surgical instruments. Placing the items on a metal tray on top of a movable table, he paused and asked Bramley, "Can you get me the photographs that you took during your initial examination? I'd also like to see the photos of where the body was found."

Bramley retrieved printouts of the photos and handed them to Symington.

Symington carefully studied the pictures. He then performed a thorough examination of the woman's mouth and nasal passages. Finding nothing new, he made an incision on the side of her neck an inch or so behind the ear, just below the hairline.

Bramley was a bit puzzled by this and asked, "What do you hope to find on the back of her neck?"

"This will give me sufficient access to look at internal bruising on the neck and will be appreciated if there is an open-casket funeral."

"Very considerate of you. Just one more reason it's nice to have you here."

Symington quickly confirmed death by strangulation. He also found extensive bruising and signs of internal bleeding in her chest and stomach areas.

"There's no doubt in my mind that she was beaten, then strangled. Most likely by a garrote made of half-inch rope."

Turning to Ernesto, he asked, "Can you please take three photos of her neck from all sides, and the stomach area, both inside and out? Take some shots of her upper arms as well."

Ernesto dutifully began clicking away with his digital camera. When finished, he looked at Symington expectantly, "Anything else?"

"I'll lift some more fingerprint samples. And, Jim, can you please draw another half-dozen blood samples? Oh, yeah, before I forget: Will you take some shots of her wedding rings, Ernesto? That looks like an expensive, custom-made set to me. Perhaps a jeweler will recognize his handiwork.

"That reminds me, Symington continued, "we need to do a full dental panel on her."

"I can have our dentist do that or have him set up the equipment so that you can,"

Bramley replied.

"It'll be quite okay if he does the panel."

"I'll have him put them on the computer so you can access them at any time and forward them as needed."

"Well, that pretty well wraps it up. Do you have a clerk onboard who can input my notes on the computer? If I have to do it, the cruise will be over before I finish."

Bramley nodded and stepped to the door. Opening it, he motioned to someone to come in.

"Miss Klemenic, I believe you've met Dr. Symington?" She nodded and he continued. "Dr. Symington has been kind enough to lend us his expertise and performed an autopsy on our Jane Doe. Would you call the Purser's office and see if they can spare someone for a couple of hours to help Dr. Symington with his report? He's one of the best pathologists in the business, but it seems he's a lousy typist."

"I could help him. I'm an excellent typist and I'm familiar with most medical terms. I could get one of the other nurses to cover reception."

"That would be a big help, Miss Klemenic. Is that all right with you, Bart?"

Symington quickly agreed and set up a time to meet with her. As far as he was concerned, she could take the rest of the cruise to do the report!

When Miss Klemenic left the room, Bramley looked at Symington with a wry little smile on his face and said, "Remember you're working, Bart. There is no fraternizing amongst crew except with permission of a superior officer."

"So who's her superior officer?"

"I am. So forget it!"

"Fine. I'll just go take a nice, cold shower. Wanna join me later for something to eat? Autopsies always make me hungry."

"I always knew you weren't sown up tight. I'll pass on the food. Autopsies have just the opposite effect on me. I need to go tell the staff captain about your findings and see what he thinks ought to be done next. Ernesto can join you if he likes."

"No thank you, Doctors. I need to get back to my other duties. I'll have the photo shop make you some prints and copy the disc to a flash drive for use on a computer."

EIGHT

"Hola, Patrón. Que paso?"

"Quit kissing ass, Ramon, and pay attention. I gave you and Estaban a job to do and I haven't seen anything in the news. Why not?"

"We did exactly as you told us. We went to the pig's house in Chula Vista. His wife showed up late in the afternoon. We kept an eye on her until it got dark, then went inside. When we surprised her she pulled a pistol out and shot Estaban in the arm before I could grab her. Estaban got really mad and he hit her in the stomach several times before I could stop him.

"We questioned her for over an hour about her husband, but she did not say a word. Estaban had his rope and he threatened her with it, but she still did not talk. He wrapped the rope around her neck and choked her several times. Still she didn't give us any information on where to find Arona.

Estaban started choking her again and she kicked him in the groin. He just tightened the rope and didn't let go until she was dead.

"I found some stuff in the bathroom to bandage Estaban's arm, and we cleaned everything up. I was looking for something to carry her out to the van in and found a big suitcase in a closet. When I brought the case out, Estaban had taken all her clothes off and was standing over her. I don't know what he intended to do. I yelled at him to remember why we were there and he moved away.

"We loaded her into the suitcase, put it in the van and drove down to the pier where the cruise ships dock. We dumped the case in with all the other luggage. I thought no one would notice one more suitcase. It worked; it was like no one even saw us."

"So why hasn't there been any news about a dead woman being found at the pier? I want that pig, Arona, to know we know who he is."

"I don't know, boss. Maybe they loaded it on a cruise ship with all the other luggage."

"No way. They run all the luggage through security just like the airport."

"Maybe they put it in unclaimed luggage. If so, they'll discover the body in a few days. Do you want Estaban and me to go back to the pier and see what we can find out?"

"No. You continue looking for Arona. How is Estaban's arm?"

"It's okay. I stitched him up and bandaged the arm. I also gave him some amoxicillin to fight infection. He should be fine in a week. If not, I'll send him home."

"When you find Arona, I want him alive. I need to know exactly how much he knows about our operation. Do you understand?"

"Yes, boss."

"Tell Estaban he can send Arona on a cruise with his wife after I'm finished. Tell him if he ever kills anybody again without my permission, I'll kill him."

"I'll make sure he understands."

NINE

After a sleepless night spent thinking of every possible way of tracking down his wife, Arona decided to let Harry Walters handle that job. Arona would remain inconspicuous, and reduce the chance of getting himself killed until he had a better grip on the whole situation.

"Harold Walters' office. May I help you?" Sunny Norton pleasantly asked.

"I would like to talk with Mr. Walters, please."

"May I tell him who's calling?"

"Just tell him it's the gentleman who stopped in unannounced yesterday. No names, please."

"Certainly. One moment please."

Harry picked up the phone when the intercom rang and listened as Sunny told him that Arona was on the phone. He told her to ring him through.

"This is Mr. Walters."

"Would it be possible to see you this morning?"

"I have some time at ten o'clock."

"Thank you. I'll be there."

"Any news yet?"

"I don't wish to say anything on the phone. I'll fill you in when I get there."

"Ten o'clock, then."

Over the next couple of hours, Arona spent time donning a disguise that changed his appearance from a smart, chic young Hispanic to a long-haired blond Californian with a deep tan and scruffy countenance. When he walked into Harry's office, Sunny didn't recognize him until he neared her desk and politely announced, "I have an appointment with Mr. Walters at ten."

Just then Harry opened his office door, and overhearing the man's comment, said, "Come in. You're right on time."

Once inside, with the door closed, Harry motioned for Arona to sit.

"Any news on your wife?"

"Nothing. I haven't wanted to go near our house because I believe Ramon and Estaban will be hanging around to see if I show up. Besides that, I'm afraid of what I might find if I go inside. That's why I wanted to see you this morning. Do you have someone who can go in and check things out without raising any red flags?"

"As a matter of fact, I do. His name is Forest Markham. You talked with him and Mr. Momi in Tijuana."

"Indeed I did. He's former MI5. I had him and Melvin Momi both checked out. Quite an impressive pair. How soon can you have him check the house?"

"He should be arriving in San Diego any time now. If possible, I'll have him go over to your house to take a look around later this afternoon."

"Good. I talked to Sharon's mom. She hasn't heard from her in several days.

"What about you? Can you stay out of sight while we try to figure out your wife's disappearance?"

"It all depends on how they found me out. If someone in the agency ratted me out, they'll know I was headed to San Diego to get Sharon. No one knows about my safe house, so I should be okay there for the next few days."

'When Markham gets here, I'll have him check out your house, and I'll also have him begin a routine missing persons search for your wife."

"That could tip someone off to our

whereabouts."

"Markham is very good at what he does. He knows not to divulge anything he shouldn't. Would it be acceptable to use your mother-in-law as a reason?"

"Good idea. No one is going to bother with her. She has early stages of Alzheimer's, so that would be a good idea and shouldn't put her in any danger. Here are the keys to my house for Markham. You have my burner-phone number. Call me the minute you find anything."

"I will. Are you going to the safe house?"

"There's not much else I can do for the moment."

———

After Arona left, Harry readied the information for Markham. As he worked, he let his thoughts drift to his ex-wife. He and Dayna had just recently reconciled their differences from the divorce and were back on amenable terms. He wondered if he could handle Dayna disappearing in the same analytical fashion Arona/Whitehill was with his wife. What concerned Arona more? That his wife was missing and possibly dead? Or his own safety? For that matter, it may be both. Arona had been undercover for some time now. He may still be carrying out the persona of Arona rather than being the true Kevin Whitehill. Time would tell.

TEN

Markham slowed his rental car and noted the address on the small cottage, confirming he had located the Whitehill residence. Rather than pulling into the driveway, he proceeded down the street to the corner, made a U-turn and parked in front of the house making mental notes of the adjoining houses.

Seeing no one around, he approached the house and rang the doorbell. After waiting a moment and listening for any sounds within, he unlocked the door and carefully went inside. He made sure there was no one inside, then began a thorough examination of each room. Other than being stuffy from being closed up, the house appeared normal.

When Markham entered the master bedroom, he noticed one closet door stood open. He turned on the closet light and noticed a rectangular impression in the carpet where something had sat. Next to that spot were two suitcases. They were part of a matched set of luggage. Studying the size and shape of the cases, Markham concluded that the impression on the floor was probably from a large suitcase that was part of the set. He took photos of the cases and finished his search of the house.

As he was locking up the house and getting ready to leave, he noticed an elderly couple standing on the sidewalk next door. He approached them and asked if they lived in the neighborhood. The lady replied that they lived next door. Noting the questioning looks on their faces, he introduced himself and said he was contacted by a friend of his, Mrs. Whitehill's mother, to look in on her. He carefully explained that Mrs. Whitehill's mother was suffering from Alzheimer's and was worried because she hadn't heard from her daughter in a few days. As a favor to her mother, he had agreed to come and see if she was home since she wasn't answering her phone.

The couple introduced themselves as John and Rita. They hadn't seen Mrs. Whitehill for several days. The last they noticed anyone around was the previous week when a plumber's van was parked in the driveway. The only thing they could remember about the van was that it was white and had "Quality Plumbing" on the side.

Markham thanked them and headed to his car. As he was starting the car, he glanced into his side mirror and noticed Rita looking at his car and writing in a small notebook.

"Smart old devils," he said to himself. "They're checking me out. I'm going to have to have to set up my story just in case someone gets nosey."

ELEVEN

"Allo, 'arry," Markham greeted Walters with a bit of Cockney twist.

"Hello, Forest. Did you find anything at the Whitehill house?"

"May have. There seems to be a large suitcase missing from a set in the master bedroom closet. I'll send you photos."

"That doesn't sound good. Do you think it was large enough to put a body in?"

"Yes. That's why it caught my attention. I'm also sending you photos of a couple who live next door that I managed to get on my cell phone so we can check them out. They seem innocent enough, but she jotted down my license plate number. They said there was a plumbing van at the house last week from a company called Quality Plumbing. Need to check that out as well."

"Tell me more about this couple."

"They introduced themselves as John and Rita. My guess is they're both in their late sixties or early seventies. Looked to be in good shape. Both were slender and mentally quite with it."

"Thanks, Forest. See you soon."

———————

A few moments later, Harry received the photos from Markham on his cell phone. After transferring them to his computer, he placed a call to Dr. Symington on the cruise ship.

"Well, Bart, how's the cruise going?"

"Great! Since I finished the autopsy, I've been kicking back and enjoying all the ship has to offer."

"Can you send me some photos of the suitcase the lady was found in?"

"Certainly."

"Can you also send me a photo of the lady's face?"

"Sure. What's this all about?"

"I'll explain later. Enjoy your cruise."

"Oh I am, Harry! I am!"

———————

Later that day, a knock sounded on Symington's stateroom door. He opened the door to Dr. Bramley who said, "I just got word that the FBI has ID'd our suitcase lady."

"Come in, come in." Motioning Bramley to an overstuffed chair, Symington took a seat opposite and asked eagerly, "Who is she?"

"The FBI says she is Sharon Whitehill, an undercover policewoman from San Diego. They want a full report of your autopsy and findings forwarded to them as soon as possible. They're launching a joint investigation with the San Diego Police Department."

"What about the body?"

"Ernesto is going to make arrangements for her to be shipped from Honolulu back to San Diego via military transport. The agent I talked with was pleased that we've kept this all quiet. He said it will help their investigation. He also cautioned me to tell everyone involved to keep this under wraps until further notice."

"I've already shared some of this information with my attorney friend back in San Diego."

"Well, just don't give out any more information until they give us permission."

"I understand. That won't be a problem. You seem a little unnerved. Is everything all right?"

"Just a bit of stress. The cruise line is very uptight about any bad publicity. They've been putting some pressure on me to make sure we don't get blasted in the media."

"Won't the FBI's putting a lid on this solve that?"

"It should, unless word gets out through the passengers or a crew member."

"Not much chance of that, and I'm sure as hell not going to the media."

"I know. Sorry I sounded harsh."

"Well, now that the Feds are in charge, let's get busy and see how much fun we can have on this cruise. Any good-looking women on this boat?"

"We're not allowed to fraternize with the customers."

"Well, how about the crew then?"

"You're on your own, Bart. I'm keeping my head down until we reach Honolulu."

"Suit yourself. You know where to find me if you change your mind."

"As soon as Bramley left, Symington sent a text to Harry: "Out of service until further notice."

Harry heard his phone chirp and scanned the text message. He recognized

Symington's code and knew the situation had now become official. Looking at the photos of the young woman and the suitcase on his desk, he understood why.

TWELVE

Obeying the pleasant female voice on the phone that directed him to leave a message at the sound of the tone, Harry dutifully waited, then left a message on Kevin Whitehill's phone asking for a return call as soon as possible. A few seconds later, Harry's phone rang. He noted it was a restricted number.

"This is Mr. Walters."

"You called?"

"Yes. Please come to my office as soon as you can."

"I'll be there in ten minutes."

Almost exactly ten minutes later, Whitehill was ushered into Harry's office by Sunny Norton. As soon as she closed the door, Kevin took a seat in front of Harry's desk.

"Have you heard something?"

"I'm afraid so. Could you please look at this photo and tell me if this suitcase belongs to you?"

"Yes. Sharon picked up the luggage set from a Goodwill store a couple of months ago."

"I'm sorry to have to do this. Is this your wife?" Harry asked as he slid the facial photo from Symington in front of Whitehill.

Whitehill's complexion changed to ashen gray and he held his breath. Then he began to sob heavily as he placed his hands over his eyes. He slowly regained his composure and looking at Harry through tearful eyes, nodded yes.

"I'm sorry, Kevin."

After a few moments of silence, Whitehill wiped his eyes and asked, "Where did they find her?"

"Evidently she was killed and placed in the suitcase, then loaded onto a cruise ship headed for Hawaii."

"Hawaii? How was she killed?"

"I don't have all the information yet."

Whitehill stared at his wife's photo, and with an icy countenance, looked Harry in the eyes. "I've got to get to Tijuana."

"You can't run off to Mexico. It'll only make things worse."

"I'm not running off. I'm going to find Estaban and Ramon. They're responsible for this. I know it. If you're worried about me coming back, send your Englishman with me."

Pondering the pros and cons, Harry reluctantly agreed. "Since no one has contacted you yet, I don't see why you can't go to Mexico. Just follow Markham's lead and don't do anything stupid."

"I can't make any promises."

"If they arrest you at the border, call me or have Markham call, and don't say anything until I get there. I know it's cliché, but I mean it. Keep your mouth shut."

"Yes, sir."

THIRTEEN

Harry sat quietly contemplating what he would do if he were Arona. Human nature is a funny thing. The one thing he'd learned during all his years as an attorney is that everyone reacts differently to a loved one being murdered. Harry's gut told him that Arona probably would not be eager to go find his wife's killer if he was the one responsible for it. This led his thoughts to Dayna.

"Hello, Harry. Nice to hear from you."

"Hi, Dayna. Nice to hear you as well."

"You sound a bit down. What's going on?"

"Just this damned job, I guess."

"Damned job? I never thought I'd hear you utter that sentence, Harry. How can I help?"

"I'm dealing with someone who just found out his wife was murdered. After our ordeal in Santa Barbara, I just wanted to know you're okay."

"Thank you, Harry."

"Dayna, what can you tell me about the people you met down in Mexico?"

"You still involved in that mess?"

"Indirectly. When you were around Arona, was there anyone else besides Ramon and Estaban he talked with?"

"Only the Mexican businessmen and their wives. I've already told you about that."

"Thanks. I feel better just knowing you're okay."

"And I love you, too, Harry. Oh, wait a minute! I do remember one meeting…there was an Asian man present. No names were given, but his wife was Filipino. She and I talked a lot about Hawaii. She mentioned that she and her husband visited Hawaii three or four times a year. Does that help?"

"It may fit into the puzzle. I'll just have to wait and see."

"Call anytime, Harry."

"Thanks, Dayna. Talk with you later."

FOURTEEN

Sunny Norton's cheerful voice on the intercom announced a call from Assistant District Attorney Ray Williams.

"Good afternoon, Mr. Williams. What can I do for you?"

"Well, you can tell me where Kevin Whitehill is."

"I'm afraid I don't know the answer to that."

"Come on, Harry. I shared with you. Now it's your turn."

"I know, but I really don't know where he is. He's supposed to contact me again soon, but he didn't tell me where he is. Why do you want him?"

"First, his wife has been murdered, and second, we need to find out if he had anything to do with it."

"Who is 'we'?"

"At the moment, the FBI and the San Diego Police Department."

"Okay. As soon as I hear from him, I'll have him call you. Just make sure I'm present if anyone wants to question him."

"Certainly. Did you ever talk with the DEA?"

"No. Never had the chance. Why?"

"You'll find out soon enough, I guess. Whitehill's wife was working undercover through the police department and the DEA--investigating him."

"What? His wife was undercover DEA? Where?! That could certainly complicate matters."

"Just one more reason we need to talk with Whitehill."

"Understood. You have my word. I'll have my client contact you as soon as possible."

"One more thing, Harry. One of my police contacts told me this morning that the DEA was asking about that English spy you've got working for you. Anything you want to share?"

Harry thought to himself, "It's a good thing Forest told me about the old couple taking note of his license number."

"No big deal, Ray. I had Forest go to Whitehill's house and check things out. For what it's worth, he didn't find anything. And before you ask, he didn't touch anything."

"That's good because it's now a crime scene and off-limits."

"You're telling me Mrs. Whitehill was killed there?"

"Her body was found stuffed in a suitcase on a cruise ship. The suitcase is from a set found at the Whitehill's residence. The body is being shipped back from Hawaii and will be in San Diego police custody in about five days. Your old buddy, Dr. Symington, did the autopsy on the ship, but don't try to get any information from him. The FBI has put a full gag order on his findings. You'll both face obstruction charges if you violate the order."

"Thanks for the law lesson, Counselor. I'm fully aware of the consequences of messing with FBI investigations. Are they handling this case?"

"Right now, it's a joint operation with the FBI and San Diego police. That may change depending on what all is behind this. You can bet the DEA will be in on it."

"Thanks for the heads up, Ray. I'll ask Whitehill to contact you as soon as I can."

"Okay, Harry, and since this may be our last little unofficial conversation, I also want you to know that I've got someone looking into the DEA's connection to the Whitehills. There's something going on there."

"See you in court."

"Most likely."

FIFTEEN

Melvin Momi was sitting in his car on Kalakaua Avenue keeping an eye on one of the local drug dealers when his cell phone rang.

"Aloha, Ernesto. How is everything on the party boat?"

"Not much of a party at the moment, Melvin. I need your help. Do you still have some sway with the military?"

"Depends. Why?"

"I need to have a body flown back to San Diego without anyone finding out."

"What? Did you go nuts and kill someone?"

"No, no. Not me. Someone killed a woman and dumped her in a suitcase that was loaded on the ship. The FBI and cruise company both want it kept quiet. I mentioned to the FBI that I knew you and said I would contact you."

"I see. Why doesn't the FBI just take

care of this themselves?"

"Too many people involved and there could be a leak. I told them you had people you could trust."

"Let me see what I can do, but I'm going to need a written release for the body for my files. I don't want some Fed conveniently forgetting that they gave me approval. Same for the cruise company. When are you going to be in port?"

"Four days. I'll keep you posted on the exact time and pier location."

"Is this the number you want me to call you back on?"

"Yes. This is my private cell phone."

"I'll get back to you in the morning."

"Mahalo, my friend."

"A hui hou, Ernesto."

Melvin continued his surveillance of the drug dealer and took numerous photos of his latest transaction. Melvin was assisting the police drug task force in tracking down dealers who were becoming more and more difficult to find. With Melvin's help, the task force had uncovered the fact that most of the mid-level dealers were homeless. Not only were they difficult to keep track of, but they were using government-supplied cell phones and bus passes to stay in contact with each other and get around. Melvin had compiled a list of over twenty such dealers and today's target would be added to the list. The task force planned a mass arrest as soon as they knew what they deemed to be the majority of players.

All of this reminded Melvin of Ernesto and himself tracking down contraband dealers when they were in the Army Criminal Investigation Division. Ernesto was a good man and extremely secretive. That was one of the main reasons Melvin used him on most clandestine missions.

Melvin called the CID office at Schofield Barracks and asked to speak to Major Denton.

"Major Denton's office. May I help you?"

"Hi, Kalie, is Denton available?"

"Hi, Melvin. He sure is. Just a moment."

"Melvin," Denton answered cheerfully. "Nice to hear from you. You still rounding up drug dealers?"

"Got another one today. You should be reading about us in the paper soon."

"What can I do for you?"

"Glad you asked. I need a body

airlifted back to the mainland."

"Anyone we know?"

"No. This is a hush-hush for the FBI. You remember Ernesto Lopez?"

"Sure. He retired to a cruise ship, didn't he?"

"Yeah, and he found a dead body in a suitcase that needs to be delivered quietly to the San Diego police."

"I see. So, we have the papers to go with the body?"

"We'll have them all signed and sealed by the FBI very soon."

"Why are they involved?"

Melvin relayed the entire story to Major Denton and the reasons to keep everything quiet."

"We can take care of it. Since we sometimes transport bodies for the airlines, no one should take notice. Come by sometime. It's been a while since we talked."

"Good idea. Thank you."

SIXTEEN

Arona and Markham were sitting at the kitchen table in Arona's safe house. Markham sat quietly sipping a cup of tea while listening to Arona talk about his wife.

"I just can't believe she's gone. Why didn't they kill me?"

"Sometimes what happens to us just doesn't make any sense. I lost a lady I loved very deeply because I made a mistake in judgment. It has taken years to accept that, and I may never get over losing her."

"Sharon and I had so much planned for the future. We both understood that working undercover was dangerous, but we never thought something like this would happen. "I was trying to set aside enough money for us both to quit police work and go somewhere we could start a family and new careers."

Tears welled up in Arona's eyes and he paused for a deep breath. "Bastards! I'm

71

going to kill everyone who had anything to do with Sharon's death. We need to go to Tijuana and find Ramon and Estaban."

"All in good time. We need to plan how we're going to find them and what we're going to do when we catch them. Killing them may not be the best option. You may need them alive to help prove you didn't kill Sharon."

"So you don't think I killed her?"

"I knew you weren't a killer when I first met you in Mexico. My money is on Estaban. That man has no soul. Believe me. I know what it takes to kill someone."

"You're right. I've never killed anyone, or for that matter, I've never had anyone killed. So how do we get those two?"

"First, we find them. That means going to Mexico. Then we need to figure out how to get them back here alive. We also need to do it quickly. There's going to be a lot of people looking for you."

"No one is aware of this disguise or the passport that goes with it. I've never used it before. Do you have alternate papers?"

"No need. You go separately and I'll meet you at that little bar by the bull ring. It has the puke green façade with all the really bad signs."

"I know it well. It's a sailors' dive bar. You can get anything there from an STD to information."

"Good. Now let's coordinate our phones and exactly how we're going to go about this. Do you have a weapon?"

"Two. Why?"

"Give them to me. They'll be hard to get across the border. I can always get new ones on the other side."

SEVENTEEN

Brenda Carlson, Regional Director of the Federal Drug Enforcement Agency, entered her office to find a good looking young man waiting for her. Pausing just inside the door, she looked at the man and said, "May I help you?"

"Are you Brenda Carlson?"

"Yes, and this is my office." Taken slightly aback by the curt question, she asked, "Who are you and why are you here?"

"I'm Special Agent Davis with the FBI," he replied, showing his credential wallet and badge. "I need to talk with you regarding two of your agents."

Leaving him standing, she asked, "Which agents, and why?"

"Would you mind if I shut the door? This is for your ears only."

Noting the young agent's deadly serious demeanor, Carlson walked over, shut the door, and motioned for Davis to sit. "The floor is yours, Agent Davis."

"Thank you. I'm here to inform you that your agent, Sharon Whitehill, has been murdered and that her husband, Agent Kevin Whitehill, is being sought for questioning. The FBI would appreciate any information you may have on the Whitehills."

"Enough of the ego trip, sonny. I've been at this longer than you've been alive. So, cut the bullshit and tell me how and when she was killed and why you want her husband."

A bit embarrassed, Agent Davis blushingly replied, "I'm sorry, ma'am. I was just trying to appear official. I have this packet from our regional director that should answer your questions. I was told to also give you this phone number to call the director privately if you have further questions."

Carlson opened the packet and began to read. A few moments later she looked up at Davis. "Thank you, Agent Davis. You've been instructed to forget this meeting and anything related to the two agents, haven't you?"

"Yes, ma'am."

"Good. You may go now."

Carlson re-read the details of Sharon's body being found, then asked her secretary to bring her several files pertaining to the drug cartel in Tijuana and Ensenada. After reviewing the files, she asked her secretary to contact Ben Atwood, one of her senior staff, and have him report to her office. Noticing Chris Walden at his desk, she walked to him and said, "I need you to step into my office."

Walden closed the file he was working on, placed it in his desk drawer and locked it, then followed Carlson to her office. "What's up, Director?"

"I've got a special assignment for you and Atwood. I want you two to track down Kevin Whitehill and bring him back to the office."

"Do we need to know why we can't just call and have him come in?"

"I'll fill you both in as soon as Atwood gets here. In the meantime, pull all of Whitehill's files and learn all you can about him. You, Atwood, and I are the only ones to know about this."

"Yes, ma'am," said Walden, and returned to his desk.

Carlson unlocked a large file cabinet in a corner of her office and withdrew a sizeable file labeled Whitehill, S/K. She took the file to her desk and spent the next half-hour reading the entire file. When she had finished, she took two handwritten pages out and ran them through the shredder.

Shortly thereafter, Agent Atwood entered Carlson's office with Agent Walden close behind. Shutting the door, he matter-of-factly asked, "You wanted to see me? You know what I'm working on. I hope this is more important."

Atwood was a seasoned veteran and probably would have been director except for the reigning politics, so Carlson allowed him to vent without retort. "I do. Ben," she said, trying to soften the situation. "We have a potential bomb facing us and I need you to help me defuse it."

"A bomb?" Atwood said in startled voice.

"A political and career-shattering bomb. You both know the Whitehills."

They both nodded.

"Sharon Whitehill was murdered a few days ago. Her body was found stuffed in a suitcase on a cruise ship. The San Diego police and FBI are launching a joint investigation and I am requesting they include us. Knowing the FBI, that may or may not happen. What I need you two to do is find Kevin and get him back here as soon as and as quietly as possible. He was in deep with the Tijuana cartel. If they found out he was DEA, they may have killed Sharon. You have all the information I have in those files and my authorization to do whatever necessary to bring him in, preferably alive. Any questions?"

"Just one," said Atwood. "You know Kevin knew you were using his wife to birddog him, don't you?"

Acting nonchalant, Carlson replied, "I suspected he did. Just another way to keep things under control."

"You like the control, don't you, Brenda?"

"Don't be insubordinate, you big ass. That mouth is the main reason you're not in this chair. Also, this is to remain top secret amongst us. Am I clear?"

In unison both men said, "Yes ma'am."

EIGHTEEN

The diminutive Asian man sat quietly at the table with his hands pressed together at his face as if in prayer carefully listening to the Mexican drug lord.

"Mr. Truong, we have salvaged ninety-five percent of the shipment to California and Hawaii. The other five percent is being held until we can rebuild the Tijuana connections we lost with the disappearance of Arona."

"How long until that conduit is restored?"

"Two weeks. Twenty days at the most. Even sooner if we find Arona and determine how much he knows."

"Killing his wife was not a prudent move. Now we have very little leverage against him."

"An error on my part that I will correct as soon as I no longer have use for Estaban. At the moment, he and Ramon are my best chance of locating Arona."

"Assign Ramon the task when the time is right. It will be a good test of his loyalty and serve as an example for others."

"Consider it done. Is everything in place for Hawaii? Our shipment from Honduras will be ready in two days."

"I've rebuilt our network on Oahu. Our old friend, Mr. Momi, has been helping the task force locate a lot of our distributors, but we have an almost endless supply with the homeless there. The government is pushing to ban them from the tourist areas because it is affecting tourism, especially the Japanese. If they are successful in putting them in temporary housing on Sand Island, our access to Waikiki will be reduced. We may have to go back to using the bellmen and concierges at the hotels. By the way, how did you find out that Arona was an agent?"

"Estaban noticed Arona frequenting a small bar near their office once a week. Estaban had a relative follow him into the bar and watch him. The relative told Estaban that Arona gave the bartender an envelope and some money. Estaban and Ramon picked up the bartender and forced him to turn over the envelope. It contained a large wad of cash for his wife and a report to the director of the

DEA in San Diego."

NINETEEN

"Aloha, Harry. How are things in California?"

"Much like Hawaii, I presume. What's Mr. Momi up to today?"

"A lot of procedural work for our forensic buddy. Have you talked with Bart lately?"

"Just briefly. He told me about the body on the ship, then I received a text saying he couldn't talk anymore. Are you helping him?"

"As I mentioned, just some procedural work. I can fill you in in a couple of days."

"Did you have another reason for calling?"

"I do. You know I've been doing all I can to uncover Truong's drug operation here on the Islands. When I heard about this body on the ship, I remembered that there was a similar killing here three months ago. A woman was found in a shipping crate. Turns out she was the main squeeze to a drug dealer who was skimming money. I don't know if the two deaths are related, but I think it's a pretty strange coincidence. I was wondering if you or Markham have heard anything through the grapevine."

"I respectfully decline to answer."

"Wow. Did the FBI put a gag order on all my friends?"

"Some of them. Speaking of friends, how are Tyler and Mei Li doing?"

"Never saw a happier couple in my life. Oh, and Honey Boy and Patty are up to their necks in wedding plans."

"That should make for a loud and interesting marriage."

"Yeah. I hear that. Well, call me back when and if you can talk. In the meantime, I'm going back to my stakeouts."

TWENTY

Markham was sitting in a booth near the back of the bar in Tijuana where he agreed to meet Arona. He was slowly nursing his second cerveza when Arona walked in. Arona carefully surveyed the bar and its occupants before going to Markham's booth.

"Any problems at the border?" asked Markham.

"Just very long lines. The border patrol was so busy, I don't think they cared who crossed as long as they hurried."

"That's good. You want a beer?"

"No. I want to find Estaban and Ramon."

"Where do you want to start?"

"There's a bar, not too far from here, where they hang out. If we're lucky, we'll find them there. Do you have a rental car?"

"No. I used a taxi. How about you?"

"I used a taxi as well. Tijuana taxi drivers learned a long time ago to never remember a face or where they took their fares. The cops don't get any information out of them and the bad guys never know who the driver may be helping."

"Well then, let's grab a taxi and head over to this bar you're talking about."

———————

Stepping out of the taxi a few blocks from the bar, Markham and Arona agreed to use opposite sides of the street and approach the bar slowly. The tourist crowd was light, and since it was late afternoon, there weren't a lot of people going in and out of the bar.

Markham went in the bar first, and seeing no sign of Estaban and Ramon, took a seat at the left end of the bar. Arona came in a few minutes later and spotted Markham who shrugged at Arona indicating that Ramon and Estaban were not there.

Arona went to the right side of the bar near the bathroom doors and ordered a tequila. Before he could finish his drink, Ramon and Estaban entered through the back door near Arona. Neither Estaban nor Ramon recognized Arona in his new disguise and walked right past him. They loudly ordered cervezas from the bartender and sat down at a table in the center of the room.

It didn't take long for Ramon to spot Markham. When he did, he leaned forward and said something to Estaban who rose and started toward Markham. Ramon got up and approached Markham from the other side. Markham watched as the pair got closer, but showed no alarm at seeing them. Checking to see that Arona was in position, he blithely greeted the Mexicans.

"Hola. How are my two favorite Mexican errand boys?"

Estaban responded, "You got a big mouth, English. Maybe I shut it for you."

"Actually, I'm looking for you two chaps. Have a seat. I'll buy you a beer."

Both men moved closer to Markham and menacingly glared at him.

"We don't want your stinking beer, Gringo," said Estaban. "Why are you looking for us?"

Markham knew he had to act fast to calm the situation, so he bluntly stated, "I'm still looking for

Arona and the money he took. Since you two are probably doing the same thing, I thought we might be able to share some information. Have you seen him lately?"

"We wouldn't tell you if we had. Why

don't you take your English ass back across the border and stay there? It will be a lot healthier for you."

"Okay by me. Just don't expect me to share if I find the money."

Markham rose slowly and the two Mexicans backed away from him. He cautiously walked to the front door and bid Ramon and Estaban farewell with, "Hasta la vista, compadres."

Just outside the door, he stopped and withdrew his pistol waiting for the Mexicans to follow him out. Glancing back in the bar, he noticed the pair headed for the back door. He hurried back in to Arona and together they followed Ramon and Estaban to the alley where they had parked their vehicle.

Ramon opened the passenger side door and looked in the door mirror. That's when he saw Markham and Arona following them. He alerted Estaban, both of them drew their guns. Estaban fired first nearly hitting Arona. Fortunately there was a dumpster nearby and Arona and Markham ducked behind it for cover. As Markham and Arona began returning fire, the Mexicans fired several more shots, then sped away in their car.

"Well, that didn't go as planned. What

do you want to do now?" Markham asked Arona.

"You head back to San Diego. I don't think they recognized me so I can stay on their tail."

"You don't get rid of me that easily. Harry wants you back and I'm here to see that you return, so consider me your shadow."

"Then we need a car. We can't chase after them in a taxi."

TWENTY ONE

Unbeknownst to Arona and Markham, Atwood and Walden had observed the brief gunfight. They watched closely as Arona and Markham hailed a taxi. The pair followed them to a car rental agency near the border check station, then continued following them as they drove off.

"We've located Whitehill. He and a companion just exchanged gun fire with two Mexicans. It looks like he's going to be here a while. I'm sending you photos of the two Mexicans. Get me what you can on them," said Atwood. "From what we've just seen, Whitehill is after them. We just need to find out why. He's either trying to shut them up or they know something."

Brenda Carlson listened to Atwood describe the situation in Tijuana, then asked "Do you need more help?"

"Not yet. If they head north, we may."

"Just got a hit on your photos. Those guys are Estaban Ramirez and Ramon

Archuleta. They worked with Whitehill and are connected to the cartel. I'm sending their last-known addresses and frequented locations. Try to intercept Whitehill and get him back here, but be careful. The man with him is Forest Markham, a former British spy. He works as a private detective. I have no idea why he's with Whitehill, but all of our records indicate that he can be deadly!"

TWENTY TWO

Melvin Momi was sitting in his car observing another drug deal go down and carefully taking photos and notes. He waited until the tourist, who bought a few small packets of marijuana, left. Then he stepped out and approached the dealer.

"Tommy, what the hell are you doing?"

"Just getting by, man, just getting by."

"When did you start selling junk?"

"A couple months ago. Had some medical problems and no money or insurance. I had to do something, man. I don't sell anything but weed. They don't want me pushing the hard stuff. That's for the big guys."

"What big guys? Who are you working for?"

"No names, Brah. I just get a new phone every week with one number on the contact list. I call the number and a voice tells me where to pick up the stuff along with an address of where I'm to drop off the money and pick up my new phone."

"You're too dumb to be doing this, Tommy. Let me help you find a different job."

"Okay by me, Captain. I just need a way to make some money."

"I'm not your captain anymore, but I'll see what I can do. In the meantime, I want you to find out if anyone knows anything about who is killing off the drug dealers' wives."

"Everybody's talking about it. They say it's punishment for people skimming. Some Asian badass is the Big Kahuna now, and everybody is afraid of him."

Melvin thought to himself, "Truong. It has to be him." Recalling how his own wife died, and how several other women were killed, he knew it was the same MO and that Truong was responsible. "I'll get that bastard if it's the last thing I do," he vowed to himself.

TWENTY THREE

"Tyler, I need your help," said Melvin.

"We going to California to work for Harry again?"

"No. Just a little off-the-books transfer of a body when a cruise ship comes in."

"What do you want me to do?"

"Crowd control and keep me company."

"Aw, that's nice, Boss. I didn't know you were lonely."

"If that were the case, I would have asked Mei Li. She's a much better conversationalist."

"Yeah, but I'm a better listener."

"True. Enough of this, however. We just have to get the body quietly to Wheeler so they can get it back to San Diego. Have you got any new leads on Truong?"

"I just picked up some talk story last

week that there is a big reshuffle on how drugs are being distributed here on the Islands. Sounds like another big shipment is on its way."

"Have you heard about any new deaths?"

"Just one. A guy over Kanehoe found his wife and two kids in his garage. Police say the mom killed the kids and herself by putting a hose in the exhaust and shutting up the garage. The street talk, though, was that the dealer was taking money and junk from his supply to sell on his own. No one has seen him since."

"Probably Truong's doing. That's the main reason I want you to help. As usual, you and Mei Li need to stay alert."

"Don't worry. We are. The other thing I picked up on this week is there has been a sizeable increase in drug use and arrests each time a cruise ship comes in port. That's pretty normal. What's different is the talk that someone on the ships is smuggling in the dope.

TWENTY FOUR

Ernesto called Melvin to give him the details for picking up Sharon Whitehill's body.

"We will be docking by Aloha Tower about six-thirty tomorrow morning. Port Authorities should clear us by seven-thirty and passengers will begin disembarking at that time. You can pick her up at eight fifteen at Section G. She will be offloaded after all other luggage for passengers who won't be continuing on the cruise. She will be in a body-bag and hermetically sealed shipping casket. The suitcase she was found in is also sealed to protect any evidence, and will be attached to the casket. I'll meet you personally to give you the paperwork."

"I'm bringing Tyler to help."

"Tyler is that mountain, isn't he?"

"That's him. As it turns out, he can probably just carry the case and casket out like someone would a regular piece of luggage."

Melvin proceeded to tell Ernesto about Tyler's suspicions of drug smuggling on the cruise ships, and requested any information on the body as soon as he could release it.

TWENTY FIVE

Ernesto and Popindreau were going over the checklist for dispatching the body the next morning.

"Are you sure no one besides you, the captain and I know about our plan for tomorrow morning?" Popindreau inquired of Ernest.

"As positive as I can be. Unless there is a leak by the FBI or one of us, no one else except Momi knows, not even Dr. Symington. He has been told that the body will be sent out in a shipping casket. Once the body is safely back in San Diego, he will be contacted to go in and reaffirm his autopsy with the medical examiner. Since he will be on the cruise until we return to San Diego, that gives them nine days minimum to get everything together at the other end. I will personally seal the casket, and then have Symington watch over it until the local funeral home picks it up to take it to the airline. Momi has assured me that the body will be kept under refrigeration and that his Army contact is very trustworthy. Our friend with the FBI has given me assurance that their records will show that the body was discovered on the pier and had nothing to do with the cruise ship."

"Excellent, Ernesto. I'll see to it you are rewarded for your efforts."

"Thank you. But you realize we didn't do anything wrong?"

"Of course, but publicity with something like this is always negative. One little blip on the radar can cost us thousands of dollars."

"Oh, I know. Perception far too many times becomes the reality.

"Can we discuss how to go about our investigation of how the body got on board? And any possible chance we have someone on board trafficking dope?"

Over the course of the next half-hour, Popindreau and Ernesto laid out several scenarios as to how the body got aboard. They narrowed the list of crew involved down to three Indo-Chinese. A surveillance plan was drawn up, then Popindreau returned to the bridge to report to Captain Stephalos.

TWENTY SIX

While Harry was waiting for Arona and Markham to return from Tijuana, he opened his laptop and began a pre-trial notebook on Arona/Whitehill. Just the fact that he was using a double name on the folder caused him a bit of trepidation. The notebook was something he learned to put together early on to help him recall even the most minute detail. Sometimes it is months, or even years, before a case actually comes to trial, and the notebook was the key to Harry's success.

As he began to organize what information he had into categories, he recalled the often-quoted saying of his favorite law professor: "Even the dullest pencil has a better memory than the sharpest mind."

The first three folders he created were: Client Notes, Possible Charges, and Investigative Notes. He thought for a moment, then added a fourth folder: Jurisdictional Involvement. He mulled over the fact that if Arona was arrested, he would be facing a three-pronged attack from the FBI, the DEA and the SDPD.

He called Sunny into his office and asked, "Would you see if you can get ahold of Markham? I haven't heard from him now for two days."

"Will do. If he's still in Mexico, he won't respond. He never turns his phone on when he's down there. He claims the Federales track all American cell phones."

"I doubt that, but he's the spy."

After completing his notations in the pre-trial notebook, Harry shut down the laptop and told himself that he needed more information on the DEA operation and involvement.

TWENTY SEVEN

Assistant District Attorney Ray Williams and San Diego Police Department Chief of Detectives Bob Halbertson had just finished an hour-long review of all the information they had on Sharon Whitehill. Williams sat back in his chair and asked, "Well, Bob, what do you think? Do we arrest Kevin Whitehill or not?"

"Damned good question. On the surface, he's the prime suspect. But I get the feeling you have the same gut reaction I do. Namely, that there's a lot more to this than we know."

"You're right. I understand the FBI stepping in, but the DEA part of this is a great big can of worms. I get the sense that no one in the DEA trusts anyone else.

"Have you talked with Brenda Carlson?"

'Briefly, but not much substance. How about you?"

"I'm supposed to meet with her and the FBI later today to coordinate our investigation."

"Do you think she'll tell me anything if I call and ask what Arona's undercover assignment was?"

"It will be minimal, if she does. The scuttlebutt I've picked up is he was embedded in the Tijuana cartel. If they have other operatives down there, they'll want to keep them dark."

"So do we let this play out for a while before we arrest Arona?"

"Does he even know his wife is dead? Presuming, of course, that he didn't do it."

"I don't know. So far, the strange part of all this is he contacted Harry Walters several days ago and told him he expected to be arrested for killing his wife."

"That's either damned smart or really dumb. Why would he lawyer up if he didn't do it?"

"According to Walters, Arona wanted him to find out if his wife was dead. And, if so, who was responsible? Arona's men and Walters' crew bumped heads in Santa Barbara. Arona was impressed by how efficient Harry's people were."

"I say we wait until we get better info from the Feds, unless you think Arona is a runner. He's been undercover a long time. He'll be hard to find if he wants to hide."

"Walters assured me he would have him available for questioning, so I don't think waiting will be a problem. Keep me posted on your meeting this afternoon."

TWENTY EIGHT

Brenda Carlson sat at the head of a large table in the DEA Headquarters' conference room. Her all-male audience flanked her on both sides. She began the meeting with, "Good afternoon, gentlemen. Before you is information on the apparent homicide of our agent, Sharon Whitehill. Her body was found in a suitcase on the cruise pier. Details of the autopsy and related matters are in the packet.

"What you need to know, that is not in the packet, is she was working undercover dogging Kevin Whitehill, her husband. Kevin Whitehill, also known by his alias, Rudolfo Arona, is also undercover DEA and embedded in the Tijuana and Sinaloa drug cartels. You will find my notes regarding the complications that developed after they were married, and why I think Kevin's involvement in money-laundering may be a primary motive for killing Sharon.

I must unequivocally state, however, that based on all observations they were truly in love and her death may have been at the hands of the cartel.

"I have two of my best agents searching for Kevin, and when located, will be returning him for questioning. For all we know, he may also be dead. How do we want to proceed?"

The FBI agent was the first to respond.

"Even though there may be an international tie-in, I think we can bow out and serve as support to the investigation."

Halbertson was next to respond.

"Thank you. This appears to be a somewhat straightforward homicide case with two possible suspects: the husband and the cartel. I'll be happy to follow the DEA's lead on this one."

"No, Chief Halbertson," said Carlson. "I think this will be better-served by keeping everything under your purview. If you maintain this as a possible domestic-violence incident, our cover and involvement may be salvaged. If it turns out the cartel killed Sharon, we can deal with that. Meanwhile, it gives me more time to clear all our assets and determine how it will affect our agents in the field."

───────────

Halbertson relayed the results of the meeting to ADA Williams and finished by saying, "I'm not sure why the Feds backed out so quickly. There's more to this than they're telling me. Regardless, we need Arona. Can you call Walters and have him bring him in?"

TWENTY NINE

Markham and Arona spent several hours searching Tijuana for Ramon and Estaban to no avail.

"We're running out of daylight, Kevin. We need to get back across the border before dark if we can. The security gets a lot tighter at night."

"I know. I've only one more contact, then we can head back. We're almost there."

Whitehill brought the rental vehicle to a stop in front of a small tourist gift shop. It was adorned with hundreds of skeletons and masks for the "Day of the Dead" celebration which was coming up soon. Walking inside, he talked with an elderly lady tending the shop. When he returned to the car, he said, "She says they're headed to San Diego to find me."

"Who is she?"

"Ramon's aunt. I gave her money for the shop after her husband was killed running drugs to Mazatlán."

"Well that simplified things. Let's head back to San Diego and let them find you."

Crossing back into the States went without incident. Markham and Arona met at the parking lot where they stowed their car and headed north. The parking attendant took the ticket and cash which Markham gave him and after giving him a receipt, raised the crossbar allowing them to exit. When they had cleared the area, he picked up the phone and called Agent Atwood.

"Two men just left in the car you told me to watch."

Atwood replied, "Thanks. Can you give me a description of them?"

"Sure. The older guy was tall and slender and talked funny. The other was a few inches shorter and looked kinda like a surfer."

"Thanks again. Glad we could do business."

"Me too," said the attendant, as he crinkled the fifty dollar bill Atwood had given him.

THIRTY

Markham and Arona went to see the first contact Ramon's aunt had mentioned. Arona had met the man in Tijuana and considered him harmless. Surprised to see Arona, Tito Alvarez asked, "Man, what are you doing in San Diego? Word on the street is the cartel has a couple of knuckle-draggers out looking for you."

"Do you know who they sent, and why?"

"Ramon and Estaban. They are telling everybody you are an undercover Federale, and they are paying good money for information to find you. If you are smart, you'll get your ass out of here."

"Thanks for the advice, Tito, but I've got a better idea. You tell Ramon and Estaban I'm hiding out in Old Town and pick yourself up some spending money."

"You want them to find you?"

"Other way around, Tito. I want to

find them. Those two may have killed my wife."

"Wife? I'm very sorry. What happened?"

"Someday, when I've got more time, I'll fill you in. Do you have any idea where they're staying?"

"Yeah. That Holiday Inn tourist hotel down by the 'B' Street pier."

"Muchas gracias, Tito. You're a good man," Arona said as he shook Tito's hand, slipping him a hundred-dollar bill.

Markham walked back to the car with Arona and asked, "How much time do we have to set up the trap? You do want them alive, don't you?"

"Only until I find out who killed Sharon and why. I've got a spot in Old Town by the 'Coyote' that should serve our purpose. Two hours should give us enough time."

"I'll call Harry and bring him up to speed."

THIRTY ONE

Arona's location in Old Town was nearly the perfect setup for a trap. The apartment was on the second floor of a building near the Coyote Café. Visually, it had vantage points on all four sides. Any approaching vehicles only had two access streets. And as far as anyone could tell from the outside, only a long stairwell provided entry. What could not be seen was an old service elevator that still worked. Markham surveyed the location and complimented Arona on the setup.

"Nice location, but it's a bit of a rabbit hole. Where does this exit?"

"A small alcove behind the restaurant by the dumpsters. I've used it before and we have good cover for an escape. I'm hoping we can use the elevator to trap our friends."

Unknown to Arona and Markham, Agents Atwood and Walden had tracked them all the way from Tijuana. They watched as Arona and Markham climbed the stairs and entered the apartment.

"What do you think, Atwood? Should we try to contact him now?"

"No. It's obvious they came directly to this spot. Let's wait and see why."

Fine with me. You want a taco?"

"No. And it would be better if you paid as much attention to the job as you do to your ever-enlarging stomach."

"You're no gazelle yourself. I'm getting something to eat. I haven't had anything since this morning, remember?"

When Walden returned with his sack of tacos and a cola, he also had a coffee that he set in front of Atwood. Here you go, Chuckles. Maybe this will improve your humor."

Atwood nodded and sipped the coffee. "I've been thinking. There is no way Whitehill would use a spot like this unless he was using it for a trap. We need to see if we can spot anyone watching them."

Walden finished his last taco. He was wiping the grease from his hands when Atwood came to full attention.

"There! See that? That's the third time that car has been by here. Hand me the glasses."

As the car passed again, Atwood focused the binoculars in on the occupants. "That's a couple of Mexicans I've seen before. Their names are Ramon and Estaban. They're connected to the Tijuana cartel. I'll bet even money that's why Whitehill has drawn them here."

Walden checked his revolver and joined Atwood as he exited the car and began walking toward Arona's hideaway. Ramon and Estaban parked on the side street in front of the apartment and passed Atwood and Walden on the sidewalk, mistaking them for a couple of chubby tourists headed for their next meal. As the Mexicans neared the bottom of the staircase, Atwood and Walden stepped up behind them and stuck their pistols in their ribs. In a hard, cold voice, Atwood said, "Don't move or you're both dead."

The Mexicans froze in place and remained stationary as the two agents removed their weapons and handcuffed the pair. Atwood directed them toward his vehicle. He told them they were under arrest and mumbled through their Miranda rights. Being old hands at this, Ramon and Estaban remained silent as they were driven to DEA Headquarters.

––––––––––

Arona and Markham watched the ordeal take place. As the agents drove off, Markham asked Arona, "Do you know those two cops?"

"They're not cops. They're DEA Agents Atwood and Walden. They only do special assignment work for Carlson."

"So she must have some clue that our Mexican friends are up to something. Do you think they know where we are?"

"Possibly. Now what the hell do we do?"

"Let's go see Harry. He may be able to help."

When they got to the bottom of the stairs, Markham spotted an envelope tacked to the top of the railing. The name "Whitehill" was written on the outside in bold letters by a black marker. Markham handed the envelope to Kevin who opened it and read, "Kevin, Brenda wants us to bring you in. We can help you find who killed Sharon. Call me. Atwood."

Kevin handed the note to Markham and let him read it. When he had finished, Kevin said, "Looks like they've been tailing us."

"Appears so. They're good, even fooled me. Let's take the note and all we know back to Harry. He'll know best what our next move should be."

"You're right. I'm obviously not thinking clearly. I should have spotted Atwood and Walden. I barely noticed Ramon and Estaban approaching the stairs."

THIRTY TWO

Brenda Carlson sat at her desk and quietly stared at Atwood and Walden before speaking.

"Why did you bring the two Mexicans in? I sent you to retrieve Whitehill."

"My best judgment, Director Carlson," responded Atwood in a curt, clipped manner.

"Okay, Agent Atwood. Assuming that your judgment actually means something, perhaps you could expound on why."

Atwood condescended and softened his response. "We noticed Kevin and the Mexicans playing cat and mouse all the way from Tijuana to San Diego. Kevin set a trap for them over in Old Town. I decided the best way to get Kevin in here was to disrupt his trap and let him come to us. I left him a note to call me. If he does, my plan worked. If he doesn't, then we go back to running him down."

"What if he goes under again? It'll just take longer to find him."

"Not really. That English spy, Markham, is tied to Harry Walters' hip. I think you could use him to convince Kevin to talk with you."

"Atwood, you are one big pain in the ass. You know that, don't you?"

"Yes, ma'am, but Kevin is one of us. He deserves all the help we can give him."

"That's exactly why I assigned you two to the case. The FBI is pushing pretty hard because of the money laundering Kevin may be involved in. I'll call Walters and urge him to have Kevin contact me. In the meantime, you two get back out there and bring him in.

———

Markham and Whitehill had just detailed the day's events to Walters and showed him the note.

"We're running out of time, Kevin. Our envelope of "a few days" ends in the morning. The FBI, DEA, District Attorney's office and the San Diego Police Department, along with the Mexican drug cartel, are all after you. I think the safest thing for you to do is turn yourself in to the District Attorney. That would keep everything local and out of Federal jurisdiction. "I'll call Carlson for you and let her know you'll be talking with the DA. I know you don't trust her. This may all be about the laundered drug money."

"What I know about the money isn't going to help anyone. You know as much or more than I do. I want whoever killed Sharon. I don't have a problem talking with Brenda. I may even be able to get some useful information from her."

THIRTY THREE

"This is Brenda Carlson."

"Brenda, I understand you want to talk to me?"

"Kevin? Are you all right?"

"Other than having everyone trying to track me down, I'm fine."

"I need to talk with you about Sharon."

"I already know she's been murdered. Can you give me the details?"

"Kevin, I'm so sorry. Sharon was like a daughter to me."

Whitehill interrupted her and said, "I'm past that. I need to know exactly how and where she was killed and whether the two Mexicans Atwood and Walden picked up had anything to do with it."

"The Mexicans aren't talking and we don't have any leverage on them. You worked with them. Perhaps you can get them to talk."

Ignoring the indirect attempt to have him come in, Whitehill said, "Tell me how Sharon died."

Carlson read the report on Sharon's death in detail to Whitehill, and again, offered condolences after she finished. While she was on the phone, she signaled an agent to put a trace on the line to establish the location Whitehill was calling from. She alerted Atwood, but before he could leave, Whitehill told her he would be meeting with the District Attorney within the hour.

Whitehill was surprised that she didn't try to talk him into seeing her. He closed the conversation with, "If you get anything out of Ramon or Estaban, will you please share it with Walters?"

Hanging up, Whitehill turned to Harry and Markham, "She traced the call. She even closed with, 'Tell your attorney we're here to help.' I never have trusted that woman. She did give me all the details on Sharon's death, though. It had to be Ramon and Estaban. Especially the garrote. That's Estaban's trademark. Make your call, Mr. Walters. I'm ready."

Harry dialed Sunny on the intercom and asked her to call Ray Williams. While he waited, Harry requested, "Markham, I need a written account of the details of your Mexico trip and the incidents of the morning. Kevin, make a list of personal items you'll need if you're taken into custody."

When Williams came on the line, Harry greeted him. "Hello, Ray. I have Kevin Whitehill in my office and he's ready to come in for a visit. When would be a good time?"

"Give me an hour. I'm presenting preliminary motions in ten minutes, but it should only take thirty minutes or so."

"We'll be there in one hour."

———————

Whitehill used the facilities in Harry's office to clean up and change clothes. Harry was awed by Whitehill's ability to change character and personality. The man in front of him looked and acted nothing at all like Arona or the Whitehill of the past few days. Standing before him was a thirty-something professional-looking gentleman who could be anything from an attorney to a doctor.

Markham was also impressed. He looked Whitehill over and said, "When we get beyond this present spot of difficulty, I'd like to discuss you and me working together."

"Let's hope it's just a spot of difficulty as you say."

THIRTY FOUR

"What do you mean 'there was no body?' What the hell happened to it?" screamed the police detective at the medical examiner's aide who had driven an ambulance to the military air field to pick up Sharon Whitehill's body.

"Someone picked the body up before we got here. The sergeant said a medical examiner's van showed up about twenty minutes before we did, signed for the shipment, then drove away."

"Didn't he verify their credentials?"

"I asked him that question. He said the two men were dressed in county whites and had county ID tags on their lapels. Since this was a hush-hush, he didn't think anyone but the right people would show up. That is, until we arrived. What do you want us to do?"

"Ask if they have security tapes of the men and van, and if so, bring them to me."

———————

It took less than five minutes for the FBI, DEA, SDPD, DA's office, Ernesto, and Melvin to find out someone had pilfered the body. While everyone else was busy trying to place blame, Melvin called Major Denton.

"Big problem, bruddah. You got a leaky boat."

"What you talkin'?" Denton responded in Hawaiian pidgin.

"Someone stole our body when the plane landed in San Diego."

There was a noticeable silence before Denton responded. "The pilot. He's the only one I'm not sure about. Hang on a minute." After a lengthy pause, Denton came back on the line. "He'll be back in just over four hours. Meet me at the hangar and we'll have a little chat with him."

"I'll be there. I'll bring Tyler along as well."

"That should do it. See you then."

THIRTY FIVE

Brenda Carlson entered the holding area and asked to have Ramon brought to Interrogation. The duty officer unlocked the entry door, went to Ramon's cell and placed him in handcuffs, then purposefully guided him to the main interrogation room where Carlson was waiting. The officer unlocked the handcuff on his left hand and secured him to a steel bar near the table where Carlson sat. Once Ramon was seated, Carlson nodded to the officer and he left the room.

Ramon stared at Carlson. He remained quiet until she asked, "Did you and Estaban kill Arona's wife?"

"Not me."

"I thought as much. Estaban has always been dumb as a patch of moss. Now we may never be able to recover the money. I'll do what I can to get you released, but it isn't going to be easy. Until then, I want you and Estaban to say silent. You got that?"

"Si. What about the Patrón?"

"He's not happy but thinks you can still be useful. Estaban, on the other hand, may have to go."

"Let me know when."

"We've recovered the body and will dispose of it. That should help get the F.B.I. and some of the others out of the investigation. Our routes are still intact and the timeline is moving ahead according to schedule. Murder investigations tend to fade away when there is no body."

"What about Arona? He won't give up!"

"You let me handle that. He's going to be busy as a suspect for a while."

Estaban was next to be brought in to the interrogation room. Carlson let him stew for several minutes before entering the room. When she sat down, he blurted out, "When are we getting out of here?"

"You may not. Why did you kill Arona's wife?"

"It was self-defense. She shot me." Like a child trying to talk his way out of trouble with excuses, Estaban rattled on for several minutes.

Carlson stopped him. "Enough. Just shut your mouth and listen. You give us the least bit of trouble and you'll never see daylight again. If anyone else questions you, you were just here with Ramon to keep an eye on Arona. Do you think you can remember that?"

THIRTY SIX

Kevin and Harry were ushered into ADA Williams' office and offered the comfortable arm chairs.

"I'm not sure where to begin, Harry. Since I talked with you last, things have changed dramatically."

"How so?"

"The body we identified as your wife, Mr. Whitehill, has been hijacked. Perhaps we should start with you giving me an accounting of your whereabouts for the last twelve hours."

"I've been in the company of Mr. Walters and his investigator, Forest Markham."

"And the week prior to that?"

Whitehill glanced at Harry who nodded approval.

"I left Tijuana nine days ago. I was suspicious that my cover was blown and took immediate steps to get out of Mexico.

When I returned to San Diego, I tried several times to contact my wife. Getting no response, I feared the worst and contacted Mr. Walters. During the past few days, Mr. Markham and I have been trying to locate two of my Mexican cohorts to determine if they know anything about my wife. Markham and I found them and lured them to a location in Old Town, where they were apprehended by DEA Agents Atwood and Walden before I could talk to them. I had Mr. Walters call you shortly thereafter."

Williams listened carefully as Whitehill talked, then quietly asked, "Did you kill your wife?"

"No. She was the only real thing in my life."

Harry watched the ADA's reaction to Whitehill's responses and surmised that he felt Whitehill was telling the truth. Harry carefully phrased his next comment to see if his conclusion was correct.

"Why all the added interest in my client? Agency involvement seems a bit excessive for a murder inquiry."

"I've been wondering the same thing. The cruise line interest is self-explanatory, but the FBI and DEA seem to have different agendas, and they all center on Mr. Whitehill. What were you involved in that they're so concerned about?"

Whitehill leaned over and whispered to Harry. When Harry gave his approval, Kevin told the full story of going undercover and working his way into the cartel operation in Tijuana. He related the events surrounding the money-skimming by Tommy Thompson and explained how the money-laundering and drug-trafficking in Tijuana and California were set up.

Williams said, "Well, that partially explains why the FBI and DEA are so interested. But this whole thing still smells a little fishy. If you're telling me the truth, then someone in one or both agencies have dirty fingers in the cookie jar.

"My problem of the moment is what to do with you." Looking directly at Whitehill, he continued, "I can detain you as a person-of-interest in a murder investigation, or arrest you on suspicion of international drug-smuggling and money-laundering. Or I could let you go and use you as a pawn to get to the bottom of all of this. You're the only one familiar with all the players in this game. What do you suggest, Harry?"

"Kevin needs to be protected. Most

likely the people who killed his wife are after him. Can you find out why the DEA apprehended the Mexicans that Kevin was after?"

"I can try. The answer I'll probably get is they were trying to find Whitehill. Which gets us back to why do they want you so badly? And why can't you trust your own agency?"

"Brenda Carlson has always been suspicious of me. She even had my wife bird-dogging me. Sharon told me before we got married. My guess is Brenda thought I turned and was keeping a lot of the money for myself. She was partly right. I was pigeon-holing some cash, but Thompson was the one really taking the cartel for a ride. Before I could report back in, Thompson was killed. Now someone killed Sharon. Ramon and Estaban are the only link to whoever is in charge."

"My instincts tell me you would be the best person to find out who killed your wife. My better judgment is telling me to arrest you and keep you from killing someone else. Until I get a clearer picture of who is involved and why, I'm going to keep you under wraps. I'll let you go with Harry, if he assures me you'll stay in his custody.

Okay with you, Harry?"

    "I'll make sure he's a good boy."

THIRTY SEVEN

Major Denton signaled the pilot as he entered the hangar area. After a sharp salute, he said, "You want to see me, sir?"

"Yes, Captain. Please step into my office. I need to have your report on the mission."

"Of course, sir."

When they walked through the door, the pilot was surprised to see Melvin and Tyler. Denton walked around his desk and introduced the pair. "Colleagues of mine. This is Melvin Momi, former head of Army CID, and his associate, Tyler Wilson."

The pilot nodded at the two, then turned back to the major.

"Just one question, Captain: Who did you tell you were transporting a body?"

"No one, sir!"

"Our body was hijacked. The only one who could have possibly told anyone was you."

"There were three others on the flight, sir. It must have been one of them."

"I served with everyone else and trust them with my life. Now, one more time, who did you talk to?"

The captain stood silently for a moment, then replied, "Besides the others on the flight, the only people I talked to were the transport driver who delivered the body and the cruise ship security officer."

The major, Momi and Tyler all looked at each other. Melvin asked, "Do you remember exactly what the transport driver said?"

"Yes sir. He said a vehicle would be there from the county to pick up the casket as soon as we landed. All I needed to do was hand the driver the envelope he gave me and everything would be covered."

"Did you get the driver's name?"

"No, sir. His nameplate was something like Alvarez. I may have his photo on the cargo bay security camera."

"Until we find out whether you had anything to do with it, you are under house arrest. Now, let's go review the video."

THIRTY EIGHT

"Good morning. I'm Juan Diego Sanchez with the Mexican Consulate's office. May I speak to Director Carlson, please?"

"Do you have an appointment?"

"No. But I would appreciate it if she could spare me a few minutes. I understand you have detained two of my countrymen and I would very much like to speak with them."

"One moment, sir."

The receptionist dialed Carlson's office and relayed the information to Carlson's secretary who in turn relayed the information to Carlson.

"Director Carlson will see you now, sir. Come this way."

"Good morning, Senor Sanchez. How may I help you?"

Sanchez flashed his credentials and responded, "I understand you have Ramon Archuleta and Estaban Ramirez in your custody."

"We do. We are questioning them in regard to a homicide and possible involvement with international drug smuggling."

"Have they been formally arrested and charged?"

"Not at this time."

"Then I respectfully request that they be released and allowed to return with me to the consulate."

"I will release them if you will assure me that, if we obtain further evidence that they have committed murder, you will return them to me."

"I will be happy to sign such a release document."

Ten minutes later, Sanchez, Archuleta and Ramirez left DEA Headquarters and got into a waiting limousine. In Spanish, Ramon thanked Sanchez for getting them out and added, "Tell the boss we are grateful for the rescue."

Sanchez turned in the seat and pointed a pistol right in Ramon's face. "Nobody's rescuing you, dumbass. Other people want to talk to you. I would suggest, if you want to continue breathing, that you be very honest."

Unbeknownst to Director Carlson,

there was no one by the name of Sanchez in the Mexican Consulate. Forest Markham had contacted an actor friend of his who worked part-time as a chauffeur to do a "little favor" for him.

When everyone had cleared out of her office, Carlson placed a call on her private cell phone. "Thanks for sending someone over from the consulate for Ramon and Estaban."

"What are you talking about? I don't know anyone in the consulate's office."

"Then it really was someone from the consulate, or even the FBI."

"Get your shit together, Carlson! We can't have those two talking. Find them and eliminate the problem, or else."

"You're not really threatening me, are you? That's a line you don't want to cross."

An icy response came back over the phone. "Listen carefully. You have exactly twenty-four hours to clear this matter up. Don't bother trying to call me. This number no longer exists. I will call you tomorrow. Adios, Director."

Trembling, Carlson hung up and sat at her desk for several moments before calling Atwood and Walden to start a new search for Ramon and Estaban.

THIRTY NINE

The cruise ship was approaching Nawiliwili Harbor on the island of Kauai. Ernesto and Dr. Bramley had said farewell to the body the day before in Honolulu, and life was back to normal as far as they were concerned.

Symington called Walters to have him arrange for transportation when he arrived back in San Diego. He was aghast as Harry told him about the missing body.

"That explains why the FBI sent notice to contact them as soon as I returned to the mainland. They surely don't think I had anything to do with it, do they?"

"Who knows, Bart? I'll pick you up and be there for any interrogation. Melvin called me earlier and said Ernesto Lopez may be the one who tipped someone off as to when the body would arrive."

"That doesn't sound right to me. He, Bramley and the staff captain all seemed forthright to me."

"Time will tell. Melvin is working with the cruise line and Coast Guard to uncover the drug-smuggling link from California to Hawaii. This murder may be the break they've been looking for."

"I sure hope old Bramley isn't involved. I've always thought pretty highly of him."

"I presume you have all of your autopsy notes and other items like x-rays, photos, etc., in order as you usually do?"

"Meticulously, my friend. I can go on the stand at a moment's notice."

"Do you have copies?"

"Mailed sets to my office and my home. I learned that from you, remember?"

"Thanks. That should keep someone from altering or deleting anything."

"I really don't see how they can change anything. In simple English, the lady was choked to death by a garrote one day before she was found. Everything else is just procedural background."

"See you in San Diego."

FORTY

Melvin, Major Denton and a Coast Guard security contingency boarded the cruise ship just as it was in final boarding to sail to its next port of call on Maui. Ernesto met the group at the security check station and greeted Melvin with a hearty Hawaiian handshake and chest bump.

"Colonel Momi. It's nice to see you again."

"Likewise, old friend. It's just Melvin, now."

"I know, but you'll always be Colonel to me. Thanks for your help in shipping that body back to San Diego. What can I do for you and your friends?" he asked looking over the major and Coast Guard crew.

"Can we go somewhere private?"

"Of course, excuse my manners."

A few minutes later, Denton, Momi and Ernesto were in Ernesto's office, and the Coast Guard crew were stationed outside the door.

"Okay, Colonel, why the invasion?"

"We need to ask if you gave the instructions to the pilot on where and who would pick up the body in San Diego."

"Yes, sir, I did. Why?"

Surprised by how readily he admitted to talking with the pilot, Momi then asked, "Are you aware the body was hijacked before the medical examiner could pick it up?"

"What? No! I didn't know that. What happened?"

Major Denton firmly responded, "Suppose you tell us."

"Hey, all I did was hand an envelope to the pilot and tell him it had all the papers and instructions for turning the body over in San Diego."

"Where did you get the envelope?"

"Dr. Bramley. He said everything had been cleared by the staff captain. I presumed it came from him."

Melvin then asked, "So you didn't open the envelope or see what was inside?"

"No way. It was sealed when I gave it to the pilot. He didn't even open it in front of me. Honest, Colonel, you know me. I would never do anything like that. I can't even imagine why someone would steal a body from the police."

"How well do you know the staff officer?"

"Popindreau is scheduled to become master of his own ship at the end of this cruise. I doubt he would do anything to mess that up. He's a real by-the-numbers, no-nonsense officer. He reminds me of you, Colonel."

"How long have you known Dr. Bramley?"

"This is my second contract with him. He has acted more bored with it all this trip. He was extremely nervous about the body being found and what the authorities would do. He seemed to be worried about losing his job."

Major Denton listened to Melvin's and Ernesto's conversation, then asked Ernesto to call Dr. Bramley and have him join them. Bramley entered the office after clearing the Coast Guard gauntlet. Upon seeing the major and Momi, he nervously asked, "What's going on, Ernesto?"

"These gentlemen just informed me that 'our' body was hijacked in San Diego before the police could pick it up."

"I know. I got a call from the FBI just before you called." Looking around the room, he asked no one in particular, "Do we know who did it and why?"

The major stared at him and said, "We were hoping you could tell us."

"Me? All I know is the instructions were faxed to me from the FBI. No…wait a minute. It was from the DEA. I have a copy in my office if you want to see it."

"We certainly do. Why so nervous, Doctor?"

"I took this job because I was about to lose my license. I lost a patient because I was inebriated and botched a surgery. A friend got me this job, if I promised to dry out and clean up my life. That's why I called Dr. Symington. I didn't want my name associated with a death in any way."

"Do you remember who sent you the fax?"

"Carston. No, wait. It may have been Carlson. I think her first name is Brenda."

Major Denton went to the door and motioned for one of the Coast Guardsmen to enter. "Please escort Dr. Bramley to his office so he can retrieve some paperwork for us. He is not to be left alone."

"Yes, sir. Doctor, if you will lead the way, please." Visibly shaking, Bramley left the room with his escort. Ernest, Momi and

Denton discussed the veracity of Bramley's information. They concluded that if he wasn't involved, he was definitely up to something.

Momi said, "Every time this cruise ship comes into port, we have an increase in drug activity. Maybe he's in deeper than we think. I have an idea how we can find out and maybe catch two rats in the same trap." Momi laid out his plan and the others agreed.

When Bramley returned, he nervously handed over the fax copies and said, "This is all I know about the transfer. Do you need me for anything else?"

"No, Doctor. That will be all. Thank you for your cooperation."

Relieved, Bramley exhaled loudly and left the room.

FORTY ONE

Markham was waiting at the location Arona had set up as a trap. When "the chauffeur" ushered the Mexicans up the stairs and into Markham's control, Markham passed payment to the driver. After the driver drove away, Markham handcuffed the Mexican pair back-to-back and had them sit on a rug in the center of the room. Out of curiosity, Markham glanced out to see if the limo was gone and noticed Atwood and Walden get out of their car and head for the stairs. He chuckled, "Fool me once," to himself and waited until they were nearly to the door before slipping out, catching them by surprise.

"Good afternoon, gentlemen. Perhaps you would like to join me for a spot of tea?"

The pistol pointing at their heads conveyed his request even more clearly. As they stepped inside, he took their weapons, handcuffed them back-to-back, and had them

145

join the Mexicans on the floor.

"Okay, gentlemen. Which one of you would like to start this little chat?"

Getting no response, he walked over to Atwood and directed the pistol at his left eye. "You'll do just fine. Start talking." Markham smiled, then tapped him none too gently on the top of the head with his pistol. "Perhaps you didn't hear me correctly. Start talking." Then he tapped him on the head again just a bit harder.

Atwood winced in pain and responded, "What do you want to talk about?"

"Why are you so interested in our Mexican friends here?"

"We were hoping they would lead us to their boss, Rudolfo Arona, who we suspect killed his wife and stole money from the drug cartel in Tijuana.

"Isn't he a DEA agent?"

"Yes. He was working undercover, but may have turned. A large amount of money–I'm talking hundreds of millions– went missing just about the time Arona's wife was killed and he disappeared."

"How long have you known about Arona's wife?"

"Just a few days."

"So how are these two involved?"

"They were looking for Arona. We spotted them tailing you and your partner. You got them out of our custody before we could get anything out of them."

"Do you think Arona killed his wife?"

"No. We've worked with him before. By the way, his name is Kevin Whitehill. Best cop I ever worked with." Turning toward Walden, he said, "No offense, Chris."

He turned his gaze to Markham, "Now can I ask you a question?"

"You may."

"Are you working for Whitehill?"

"Indirectly. I'm an investigator for his attorney."

"So you know where he is?"

"I do, but that's none of your concern at the moment."

"Tell him we think Carlson set him up and may be behind his wife's death. If you'll give me a few minutes with these two, I'll get the proof I need.

"No. It would be best if you just sit quietly and listen."

Markham walked to the two Mexicans and sat cross-legged on the floor in front of Estaban.

"Do you speak English?"

"No comprende."

Markham stared coldly into his eyes for a moment, then hit him across the upper lip with his pistol knocking out several teeth. Spitting blood, he gurgled out several expletives—in English. Markham continued to stare at him. "I thought that might improve your diction. Perhaps having fewer lower teeth will really improve your English."

As Markham raised his hand Estaban yelled out, "I speak English! I speak English!"

"Good. So do I. Let's talk. Why are you after Arona?"

"He is a dirty drug cop. He is stealing from the people we work for."

"So they sent you to kill him?"

"No. To take him back to Mexico so we can find out what he did with the money. Then kill him."

Markham walked around to face Ramon.

"Hola, amigo. Hablas Inglés?"

"Yes, sir, I do," replied Ramon

"I thought you the smarter of the two. Tell me your boss's name...or do you work for Carlson?"

"Carlson works for the same person we do. I don't know his name. We are given a new cell phone number once a week to call and get instructions."

"Do you know who killed Arona's wife?"

"No. We were sent here for Arona. We were told to report back any information we could pick up on her death. My guess is Carlson, or these agents, could have done it."

In a blinding flash, Markham came down with the pistol on the bridge of Ramon's nose. The crunch of bone and cartilage was sickening. Ramon screamed in pain, blood gushing from his broken nose.

"You were doing so well—right up until you decided to lie about Arona's wife."

Markham stood, walked around to Walden and addressed him. "Chris, isn't it?"

"Yes, sir."

"Do you have anything to add to our chat?"

"Only that Director Carlson had Whitehill's wife reporting to her on his whereabouts and activities. I thought that really strange."

"Thank you, Chris. Nice talking with you." As Markham walked away, Walden let out a sigh of profound relief.

Markham walked into the kitchen, called Walters, and filled him in.

"So what's next, Forest?"

"I'm going to see if the DEA guys are willing to help us. Atwood certainly doesn't care for Carlson. Walden will do whatever Atwood tells him. I'll try to keep the Mexicans alive until we get what we need from them."

"I didn't hear any of this. I think it best we don't mention anything to Kevin just yet. Do you agree?"

"Correct as usual Counselor. See you soon."

FORTY TWO

The restroom attendant entered the ladies' room near a lounge amidships and was startled to see a message scrawled on the mirror in deep-red lipstick. It read, "THERE IS A BOMB ON THE SHIP. I WANT EVERYONE TO DIE." She ran from the room and called security.

At the same time, another attendant found the same message in the locker room near the buffet. Before the attendant could report the message, two women entered the locker room together and read the message. One turned and ran out yelling, "Oh, my God! There's a bomb!" Fortunately, the music was so loud, no one heard or understood her. The attendant calmed her down, saying it was most likely a prank. She asked the two women to wait with her until security could investigate.

Security closed the restroom and locker room, and notified Ernesto. He struggled for a few minutes, trying to decide if it was a credible threat. He concluded that he couldn't take any chances. Ernesto reported the threat to the staff captain. Since the ship was nearing Kona, he could notify the police. They would have to evacuate the ship. While all the necessary calls were made, the passengers were notified that as soon as they docked in Kona, everyone would have to disembark as a required safety drill.

Amidst all the confusion of getting over two thousand passengers off the ship, few people paid any attention to the group Melvin and Major Denton had assembled. They led a team of 240 agents from ATF, Coast Guard and the police bomb disposal unit onto the ship, accompanied by fifty sniffer dogs. Twenty were trained to detect drugs, thirty trained to detect explosives.

As all the crew cleared the ship, Ernesto separated the males and females. They were questioned one-by-one, then wanded for any explosive or drug residue. Five were detained for further questioning.

Two Army CID handwriting experts sat at a table and had each female write the threat message, with both right and left hands, to see if they could find a match. An hour into the process, one young lady was arrested when it was determined her handwriting was a perfect match to the notes. Upon her arrest, she broke down and told the agents, between deep sobs, that she was pregnant by a married man and just wanted to end it all. When she was asked where she had placed the bomb, she quit talking. Major Denton ordered a double check of all passenger areas and luggage holds.

"Major, we have a positive in hold three," came a proclamation on his walkie-talkie.

"Explosives or drugs?"

"Both, sir. We're prepping for bomb removal at this time. It appears to be a small, crudely-constructed pipe bomb. Bill's suited up and is starting retrieval now. I'll let you know when it's in the safe box."

"Copy that. I want to make a big show of the removal in front of the passengers and crew so they'll feel safe about returning to the ship. I'll meet you at the gangway."

"Yes, sir. As soon as we get it safely into the lead box, we'll be on our way."

"What about the drugs?"

"It could be a major shipment. We

are just starting to open cartons."

I'll send Momi and the security chief to assist ATF with its removal."

The major turned to Melvin, "Your plan worked perfectly. They found the drugs in luggage hold three. You and Lopez go see what they have."

———

There was a gradual exit from the ship by Denton's small army. He proudly announced to all that the danger was over. He also announced that a large quantity of luggage was being taken off the ship for a more intensive search, but would be returned to the ship before it left the islands.

Hearing the announcement, Dr. Bramley immediately dialed his cell phone and reported, "I think our shipment was found and is being confiscated by the army."

"Army? How in the hell did the army find it?"

Bramley explained the bomb and all that had transpired. He then asked, "What do you want me to do now?"

"A simple suicide will suffice."

"Understood."

As the holding area was cleared, not

many paid any attention to the elderly officer slumped in a chair in the corner of the room."

———

Pulling Melvin aside, Major Denton told him, "Your former aide and her so-called bomb are being taken to Schofield. That way we won't have any problem with the news media. After this is all over, we'll clear everything with the cruise line. My guess is they'll want to take this boat into dry-dock for a while, re-crew, and start all over."

"Thanks Major. I'll make sure to stop by and thank her in person."

FORTY THREE

Truong called the Mexican cartel leader. "Our shipment was confiscated by the army in Hawaii. Some idiot put a bomb on the cruise ship. While they were searching the ship for the bomb, they found our drugs. Bramley committed suicide, and all of the crewmen involved will cease to be a problem very soon. That leaves the loose ends on your side. I want Carlson eliminated, along with Arona and the two men you sent to solve the problem."

"As soon as I can find them. Now what about our money?"

"You know the agreement. I don't pay for what I don't get. I will reimburse you twenty for your expenses."

"But I had forty invested."

"You also have your life invested, my Mexican friend."

"My apologies, my Chinese friend. I momentarily forgot with whom I was speaking. Twenty will be quite acceptable and appreciated. I will begin putting a new shipment together. You can expect delivery in Honolulu within the next ten days."

"Funds will be transferred to your account within the hour. Please keep me up to date on your search for Carlson and Arona. If you need help from my people in California, let me know."

"Thank you, sir, and again, my apology for being impertinent."

"Apology accepted."

FORTY FOUR

Carlson tried several times to call Atwood and Walden with no success. Each time Atwood's phone rang, Markham noted the number and ignored it. She tried one more time. When it rang, Markham pressed the answer button and held the phone to Atwood's face so he could talk with the caller.

"Hello, Director."

"Where are you? I've been trying to get ahold of you for several hours."

With a wry smile on his face, he responded. "I've been a little tied up. It wasn't convenient to answer the phone."

"Did you find the Mexicans?"

"Yes. I'm with them right now."

"How soon will you be back at headquarters?"

"That all depends on the nice gentleman who has a gun pointed at my head."

Markham then spoke into the phone. "Director Carlson, your agents have been very cooperative. I would deem it a great favor if you would join us, and a dire mistake on your part if you don't. You know the old TV line: 'Come alone and don't tell the cops.'"

"Why should I care about your captives?"

"You shouldn't. But you should care that if you don't, the FBI will be told of your connection with the cartel. I want information I suspect only you have. Give me what I want and you and your agents can go back to your slimy existence."

"What do you want to know?"

"Not on the phone. I want to make sure of the veracity of your answers. You need to be here for that."

He gave her the address and hung up. Walking over to Ramon and Estaban he checked their faces and saw the blood flow had stopped. He walked over to the door and announced, "I'll see you chaps later."

Taking up a position at the sidewalk bar diagonally across from the stairs, he waited patiently for Carlson to arrive.

Carlson's instinct told her that whoever she was talking to knew far more than he should. She had detected a British accent and thought it could belong to the investigator working for Whitehill's lawyer. She hadn't paid much attention to Atwood when he told her about Markham, but wished now that she had. Mulling around what he could want in the way of information, the only thing she could think of was he wanted to know who killed Kevin's wife. That she would give up easily. It would get rid of the dumb-ass, Estaban, once and for all.

"That doesn't matter," she said to herself. "I just hope he doesn't have any real information on my connection with Tijuana. If he does, I'm screwed."

Markham watched her park the car and check the address. She started slowly up the stairs and paused at the top landing before knocking on the door. Getting no answer, she knocked a little louder. She heard what she thought were voices inside saying, "come in," and carefully turned the door handle.

Only the light from the door gave any luminescence to the room. She stood in the doorway several moments letting her eyes adjust, then saw the figures of four men seated in the middle of the room. She reached toward the light switch by the door and was stopped by a firm grip on her wrist. Startled, she turned and was face to face with Markham.

"Please step inside, Director. I've been waiting for you." He shut the door, then turned on the light, still grasping Carlson's wrist in a vice-like grip. He marched her over to a straight-backed chair, frisked her and bade her to sit. Then he sat down in another chair facing her.

"Let me introduce myself, ma'am. I'm Forest Markham. I work occasionally as a private investigator. My employer has tasked me with discovering who killed Sharon Whitehill, with whom I'm sure you are acquainted. I pride myself in completing my assigned tasks. So if you will be kind enough to tell me exactly who killed her and why, my job will be finished and our business will be concluded."

"I don't know who killed Sharon. Kevin Whitehill is my primary suspect."

Markham pulled his chair a bit closer; he stared at her for a moment before saying, "Lying doesn't become you. Perhaps you should take a glance at our Mexican friends and reconsider your answer."

Atwood snorted a muffled chuckle and waited for what was to come next.

"I'll ask you one more time. Who

killed Sharon Whitehill and why?"

To Atwood's dismay, Carlson eased forward, and looking directly into Markham's eyes, began to talk.

"Since I don't have much choice, I'll take you as a man of your word and accept your bargain. Sharon was the daughter of a friend of mine. I took her under my wing and convinced her to watch Kevin. You see, several hundred million dollars, which was part of a money-laundering scheme for the Tijuana cartel, went missing. I wanted to see if Kevin would lead us to it. As far as I know, the cartel isn't aware that I know about the money.

"I have an arrangement to let an occasional small shipment come across the border, based on information I get from Kevin. When he went missing, I assumed he was going for the money and notified Tijuana. Shortly thereafter, these two showed up and I became aware of Sharon's death. So, to answer your questions, why is because the cartel wanted to send a message to Kevin by kidnapping Sharon. As to the who, he's right over there," she said pointing at Estaban. "Now can I go?"

"Certainly. There is one caveat, however. I'm going to release you into the custody of your two agents here. We wouldn't want a lady out on the streets by herself, would we?"

"Would you care to make another bargain?"

"This would be something to convince me to release you by yourself?"

"Yes. I can't give you a name, but I can give you a number for my contact in Tijuana."

"No deal. What I will let you do is lead me to your contact in person."

"How am I supposed to do that when I don't know who it is?"

"Call and see if he is willing to let you come to Mexico for protection."

"Go ahead and let Atwood and Walden take me in. If I run to Mexico, they will kill me on sight. They don't like failures."

She reached into her pocket, withdrew a cell phone and selected a number on the contact list. Handing the phone to Markham, she said, "I doubt anyone will answer. Good luck."

Atwood thanked Markham. Before leading Carlson out of the room, with Walden following closely behind, he asked, "What are you going to do with those two?"

"I'm leaving them here for the FBI with a disc from the digital recording I made of the director's conversation."

"If you get any leads on the Mexican connection, I would appreciate a call."

Markham handed Atwood a piece of paper with a number on it, then the door closed as they left.

FORTY
FIVE

Harry patiently listened as Markham gave him and Kevin a complete report on his dealings with the Mexicans and the DEA. When he finished, Harry said to Kevin, "You have your killer, and it sounds like Forest exacted a bit of revenge. Now we have to let the legal process run its course.

"I've been reviewing my files from Santa Barbara. I may have a clue as to where Thompson stashed the money. During our investigation, we found a password vault with some account numbers. I think they may lead us to a California bank. Tommy wasn't one to complicate things. I think the off-shore bank chase was a misdirection, and if so, Sandy carried off the ruse perfectly.

"Melvin called from Hawaii to let me know they made a major drug bust on the same ship Sharon's body was found. He thinks Tijuana and our old friend, Truong, are in business together. He would like to have both you and Markham join him in Hawaii to ferret things out. Kevin, I'll talk to Williams and clear you to go to Hawaii. I think he would agree that getting you a long way from Sharon's killer will be a good idea."

"I knew Estaban was probably the one who killed Sharon, but I want the one who sent him. If I can't go to Mexico, I'll go to Hawaii."

FORTY SIX

When Harry was able to talk with the ADA, Williams had already been contacted by the FBI. He had been told that Whitehill was no longer under suspicion for murder. "However, we still want to talk to him regarding his undercover work with the cartel, so he needs to remain available," Williams told Harry.

"Markham will be with him at all times. Be advised that I'm sending them both to Hawaii to help Melvin Momi. You remember Melvin, don't you? He's the investigator I used in the Thompson matter."

"Sure do. And that huge guy, Tyler Wilson. They're hard to forget! Does this have anything to do with that case?"

"It may. Momi thinks he's found a link between the Chinese and Mexicans for smuggling drugs and money-laundering."

"Chinese?" That's a new wrinkle. I've never heard of either group cooperating before."

"Momi thinks it's a shared-route setup. Each one sells different drugs, but benefit with a secure pipeline in and out of the United States."

"If he's right, I'm sure the FBI will want to hear all about it. They'll have a ball fleecing out Director Carlson."

"If the cartel doesn't get to her before they find out anything."

"There is that. Thanks for the call, Harry. Stay in touch."

———

"Well, you two are cleared to go to Hawaii. Sunny can arrange your airfare and I'll call Melvin to let him know you'll be there tomorrow. Whitehill, do exactly as Momi tells you. I'd tell you that as well, Markham, but it would be a waste of breath. Tell Tyler hello for me."

FORTY SEVEN

The Hawaiian Airlines flight was a chance for Kevin to relax as there was nothing to do for five hours. After the complimentary Mai-Tai, he nestled into the comfortable over-sized first class seat and decided to take a nap. It had been a long time since he had flown. He and Sharon had taken a few short hops to Cabo and Cancun but never first class. Melancholy set in as he thought about Sharon, then turned to rage.

Markham noticed Kevin's transition from sleepy to alert and agitated, "Everything okay, Kevin? Does flying bother you?"

"No. Just thinking about my wife."

"Kevin, it took me several years to get used to my wife's being killed. I still have the desire to kill everyone involved. I've searched Mexico for several years trying to locate those who are most likely responsible for my wife's death. I believe we are looking for the same people.

"You need to know about this fellow, Melvin Momi, we'll be joining in Hawaii. He reminds me of you in a lot of ways. He's a master of disguise and undercover work. At one time, he was the Officer in Charge of Pacific Operations for the Army Criminal Investigation Division. He retired early and became a private investigator for the sole purpose of tracking down the people who hooked his wife on cocaine. She eventually died from an overdose. Melvin has narrowed his search to someone called Truong; Melvin thinks he's the drug kingpin out of China. Truong may also be tied in with the Mexicans. Who knows, with a little luck, one may lead us to the other."

"There were several Asians who used to meet with me to set up shipments of money to be laundered. But the drugs were under the purview of the Mexicans. Tijuana was always the meeting place. The snippets of information I was able to pick up lead me to believe their center of operations is in a small village or territory that's easily safeguarded and has good transportation routes. I narrowed it down to three possible sites. Puerto Penasco, Loreto and Topolobampo. Topo is pouring a lot of money into port refurbishing, so it may be where they're loading the ships. I tracked some activity in Ensenada out of Cabo, so the peninsula may be their route."

FORTY EIGHT

Harry and Ray Williams were watching through the one-way mirror as FBI Agent Davis interrogated Brenda Carlson.

"So what you're telling me is that Kevin Whitehill stayed within the protocols of his assignment?"

"Yes."

"Will you be willing to testify to what you just told me?"

"Yes."

"Excellent, Director."

Turning to the mirror, he said, "That's enough for me. Mr. Walters, you can tell Mr. Whitehill he is free to go, and thank him for his cooperation. Now, let's talk about you, Director."

"Not without an attorney," Then she looked at the mirrored glass and asked, "Would you care to take on a new client, Mr. Walters? I understand you're one of the best in California."

Davis excused himself and stepped into the observation room. "That lady has a real set of balls, doesn't she? What do you think, Counselor?"

"Let me talk with her privately for a few minutes and I'll have an answer."

———

Carlson and Walters were escorted to a small private room with an agent posted outside the door.

"With the evidence my investigator was able to get on you, you must know you have no chance of pleading 'not guilty.' I think your attempt to hire me may just be a way to exclude me as a witness, or to suppress evidence to help your cause."

"Nothing that diabolical, I assure you. I want you to pass along a message for me. Please tell Kevin that I truly am sorry about Sharon. I loved her like a daughter. I also like Kevin and hope he really is clean. Do you know where a nasty old biddy like me can get a good attorney?"

"There are several I can recommend."

"I'm more worried about the cartel than the legal system. I just hope to hell Sonny Boy out there can protect me."

"My advice is don't say anything until you have an attorney, and be sure to tell your attorney to bargain for security and anonymity for you."

"Thank you, Mr. Walters. Be sure to tell Kevin what I said."

FORTY NINE

Melvin met Markham and Whitehill at Honolulu Airport, then drove them to the Pacific Beach Hotel where he had reserved a suite of rooms. After giving them time to unpack and get settled in, he gave them a complete briefing on the cruise ship drug bust and the information he was able to garner from the arrested crew members.

"One of the Micronesian guys was singing like a canary in hopes of not being sent home. For whatever reason, he prefers to be in jail here. The important thing is, he mentioned the big boss is on island to oversee distribution. He overheard Dr. Bramley mention the 'Halekulani' and 'Thursday.' That just gives us today to catch him."

Markham thought a moment. "Have you verified he's here on Oahu?"

"No. That will be our first task. If he is, he probably has bodyguards and lookouts we'll have to get past. He most-likely knows all our faces, that's going to be a drawback. I'll call Tyler and have him help us. He'll also give us another edge."

Whitehill interrupted, "Who is Tyler?"

Markham smiled and said, "He's Superman, Batman and the Jolly Green Giant all-in-one. I'll warn you ahead of time. He's probably the largest human you'll ever see, and he's Melvin's best friend."

Melvin added, "He's also one of the most competent operatives I've ever worked with. Tyler can scope things out, then we can go from there."

———————

An hour later, Tyler rapped gently on the suite door. Melvin rose, opened the door, and Tyler entered. He didn't say a word until the door was closed.

"Aloha, Forest. Nice to see you again."

"Likewise, Tyler."

Tyler then turned to Whitehill and stared at him for several moments. "Who's the undercover cop?"

Before Melvin could explain, Whitehill rose, extended his hand, and introduced himself. Tyler glanced at Melvin, who nodded, then Tyler stuck his massive paw out and gently shook Whitehill's hand.

"Tyler Wilson. Nice to meet you, Mr. Whitehill,"

Melvin quickly told Tyler what he wanted him to do. Tyler hurried toward the Halekulani just a few blocks away. The doorman at the Halekulani recognized him. "Aloha, Brah. What brings you into haole country?"

"Looking for a Chinaman. Got any staying here?"

"Only two."

"Where they stay?"

"One in the penthouse, the other in the oceanfront wing. The penthouse dude is a young guy into computers. The other is an old guy with body guards."

"How many?"

"Four. Two are always with him. Two are always outside the door."

"Is he tong?"

"Could be. He's dirty. He's in 207."

Tyler called Melvin and gave him the info. Melvin, Markham and Whitehill joined him a few minutes later, and they headed to the ocean wing with weapons ready. When they got to the 207 hallway, no one was there. The quartet stopped. Tyler eased toward the room. As he neared 207, the door opened and a maid with a cleaning cart came out. Tyler looked inside, then asked the maid, "Is the room vacant?"

"Yes, sir. Mr. Hong left twenty minutes ago."

"Did he say anything when he left?"

"Just that he had a plane to catch back to the mainland."

"Did he say where on the mainland?"

"Two days ago I heard one of his men say they had trouble in San Diego. Mr. Hong got very mad at the man and told him to be quiet. Then he asked me to leave the room."

"Was anyone with him?"

"He always has four men with him. They search me each time I come into the room."

"A hui hou."

"Aloha."

Melvin called Major Denton with the information Tyler had obtained and Denton put an island-wide alert out for Hong. A quick response from the FAA told him Hong had left ten minutes earlier in a private jet. The jet filed a flight plan to Lindbergh Field in San

Diego. Denton thanked the FAA contact. He called Melvin back and cheerfully announced, "We got him now! He's headed to San Diego in a private jet. We'll have the tech boys get a lock on his aircraft just in case he decides to stray from his flight plan."

"You got anything that can get the four of us to California?"

"Sure do. I can have you in the air in a few minutes. Might even be able to get you there before he lands. Get on the squawker after you take off and let me know what else you need. Once you land, get over to hangar six. Everything will be ready by the time you get there."

FIFTY

Fifty miles outside of San Diego, Hong's plane called air traffic control to begin final approach. Major Denton was notified, and he in turn notified Momi, whose plane had just landed. "Your target is less than fifty miles out. Good hunting."

"Thanks, Major. We have just enough time to get to hangar six. We can nab him when he steps off the plane."

As everyone rushed to the target area, Tyler said, "You sure taking him down here is the best idea, boss? I know you want him badly, but can't he lead us to the Mexicans as well?"

It was like a bucket of ice water to the face for Melvin. He knew Tyler was right, but here was the quarry he had spent years trying to catch.

Markham was next to speak. "He's our only link to the Mexicans. We've got all the support we need to keep track of Truong on this side of the border. Harry can get the FBI to help if we need them, but if Truong goes south, we'll be better off as a small commando force."

Kevin was next to throw in. "I'll help you put a bullet in his head, if you want. We can always go after the Mexicans."

———

Truong's bodyguards deplaned first and set up a gauntlet for Truong's exit. A quick march to a waiting limo and the troupe drove away.

As Momi and his minions were considering where to get a vehicle, a dark blue van pulled up. The driver motioned the men to get in. "Colonel Momi? Major Denton sent me. Where do you want to go?"

"Follow that car," Momi said, and chuckled out loud. He had never uttered that old cliché until now.

FIFTY ONE

Truong's entourage drove south for twenty minutes and approached the historic Hotel Del Coronado. Bypassing registration, they drove to the oceanfront villa section of the property, parked their vehicle and entered one of the units. Momi and crew watched as they entered, leaving one man to guard the entrance. A second man soon appeared on the second-story deck. That left two men inside with Truong.

Melvin turned to the driver and asked, "Do you have a contact name for me?"

"Yes sir. Commander Dawson with the naval amphibious base, just a few miles down the road."

"Can you get him on the phone? We're gonna need more eyes to keep track of our friends." The driver dialed, then handed the phone to Melvin as it rang.

"Colonel Momi? I was expecting your call. Major Denton said you might need some assistance."

"Indeed we do. So far, we haven't been spotted. Can you send two vehicles and a couple more men so we can form a tighter net around our drug dealer?"

"Copy that. I'll have them there shortly. I'll make sure they bring you some toys as well, just in case."

"Much appreciated, Commander," Melvin concluded, and told the commander where they were.

A few minutes later, two late-model SUVs pulled into the lot and parked near Melvin's location. After making phone contact, one of the drivers approached Melvin's vehicle and spoke to the driver. "Commander Dawson sent us." Looking in at Momi, he added, "Colonel, I have weapons for each of you, along with body armor and some surveillance equipment. If you would have one of your men join Ensign Velarde, you can follow me to a more secure location to transfer the items."

"Lead on, Lieutenant. Kevin, would you like to keep the ensign company?"

Momi carefully observed Truong's guards to make sure they hadn't been spotted. Then he had the driver follow the lieutenant's SUV to a parking lot next to the Coronado

Boat House Restaurant where they were able to transfer equipment.

Once back in the parking area by Truong's villa, Melvin was able to set up the surveillance plan by phone. It was a simple triangulation and afforded clear sight lines for all three vehicles, while also covering the exits.

The navy Lieutenant, in street clothes, and Markham walked over to Truong's car and deftly placed tracking devices near the license plates. Truong's men came to attention when the Lieutenant and Markham neared their vehicle, but relaxed when they concluded it was just two guests arguing about directions.

FIFTY TWO

Two hours into the stakeout, another dark SUV drove into the lot and neared Truong's villa. Ensign Velarde and Whitehill began taking photos of the three men inside the vehicle and sent them back to the naval base for a recognition search. As Whitehill watched the men through binoculars, he recognized one of the faces.

"That's Herrera."

"Who's Herrera?" asked the ensign.

"He was my liaison to El Jefe; his errand boy. He would occasionally bring me cash to be laundered and any changes in the network. He's probably here to deliver a message to Truong."

"The other two are sure giving him a lot of protection. Is that normal?"

"Not really. Maybe he's more important than I thought. Or he might have a significant delivery for Truong."

As the Mexicans entered Truong's

villa, Velarde reached into the back seat and brought out an oddly- configured piece of electronic equipment. Turning to Whitehill he said, "Let's see if we can pick up any conversation."

Whitehill watched as Velarde turned on the listening device and plugged it into a laptop so he could record what was being picked up. Next, he plugged in some ear buds and, giving one to Whitehill, they listened.

———————

"Did you have a pleasant trip from Loreto?"

"Yes, thank you. We flew into Ensenada and drove from there. Have you been waiting here long?"

"Only a couple of hours. Just enough time to relax from the flight. Let's talk about where we go from here."

"We have two days before the next shipment will be ready at all the ports. After a short pause filled with clicking and rustling noises, Herrera said, "I hope you will find this a satisfactory sample."

"Columbian?" Truong asked.

"Yes, sir. The purest high-grade we've had in several years. It can easily cut out twenty to one."

"How much will be placed on each ship?"

"Fifty pounds at Loreto, Guaymas, and Topolobampo. One hundred each at Mazatlán and Puerto Vallarta, and sixty at Cabo. The extra ten at Cabo is for the Hollywood trade."

Truong instructed his bodyguard to step into a side room and bring out two large metal briefcases. Velarde and Kevin heard the thud as the cases were dropped on a solid surface, followed by the snick of clasps being opened. "I apologize for not being able to make an electronic transfer due to the recent problem. I added an additional million to help with incidentals."

"No apology necessary. However, the incidental money will make our Customs check much easier. If you would like to spend some time at Loreto, you are most welcome to join us for the trip back."

"I would like to spend some time in Mexico. Is Mr. Ochoa going to be there?"

"I'm sorry. I am not privileged to his whereabouts."

"Intriguing. Let me take care of business here, then I'll come to Loreto."

"Adios then, amigo. Please call this

number and we will have people at the air strip to pick you up."

FIFTY THREE

Whitehill sat in stunned silence for a moment as the Mexicans left Truong's villa. Then he called Melvin to let him know what they had just heard. "We have to go to Mexico. They're both going to be in the same location at the same time."

"Patience, Kevin. With Truong staying here for a while, we'll have some time to put a plan together. We may even uncover more of his contacts in California. Do you know who Ochoa is?"

"Only by reputation. He's called El Lobo–'The Wolf.' Enrico Ochoa hasn't been seen in a couple of years and is rumored to be dead. Before he went off the map, he was the head of the Sinaloa cartel. He directed the massacre of several rival factions. When I first went to Tijuana, there was talk of a Sinaloan joining forces with the Chinese. Soon after, there were a lot of Chinese weapons being used, then things quieted down. Suddenly a faceless leader known as 'El Jefe' was in control."

"Let's go to the naval base and regroup. Lieutenant, can you have Ensign Velarde keep an eye on Truong?"

"No problem. I'll get additional manpower over here so we can keep track of their every move."

———————

Melvin, Forest, Kevin and Tyler were all seated at a table in the mess hall discussing operational plans with Commander Dawson.

"Time is a major factor, Colonel," said Dawson. "We are twelve to thirteen hours away from Loreto by land, and three or four by air. My best guess is Truong will travel by private jet. So, we need to find the best way to get you there by air. I have friends with the Mexican military in that region whom I can trust to help us. They've really been cracking down on the criminal element around Cabo in an effort to keep the Hollywood and tourist dollars coming in."

"It'd be nice if we could get there before Truong. Do you have a way to track the Mexicans so we can locate them when we get to Loreto?"

"Way ahead of you, Colonel. We installed some new equipment on their phones while they were here. There's a GPS locator, a redundant navigational feed, and satellite voice feed. All part of a courteous Customs check!"

"This new technology is something else."

"As the old saying goes, 'you ain't seen nothin' yet!'"

"How soon can you have a plane ready for us?"

"Let me make a couple of calls. It should be ready within the hour. Why don't you round up what you need and meet me back here, Colonel?"

"Thank you, Commander. And it's Momi or Melvin now."

"Yes, sir, Colonel," he replied with a wink.

FIFTY FOUR

It was an idyllic, warm afternoon in Loreto when Momi's plane touched down. The plane was met by two sedans and a small troop carrier from the Mexican army. When the plane taxied to a nearby hangar, stairs were brought up and the door opened. Waiting at the bottom of the stairway were a major and eight armed soldiers.

Markham glanced outside and quipped, "I say, Gov'nor, if they're not on our side, we could be in a spot of trouble."

"Let's go find out," said Momi, as he descended the steps.

"Colonel Momi? Major Sandoval. Welcome to Mexico."

"Thank you. Have our friends arrived yet?"

"Yes, sir. About twenty minutes ago. Two men in an SUV picked up five men and their luggage. I have people following their vehicle. We should know their location soon.

If you would please have your men come this way, we can take you to your hotel."

"Hotel? Isn't that a little too public?"

"What better way to hide than in plain sight, señor? Anywhere else, you gringos will stick out like a sore thumb." Looking at Tyler, he added, "He's going to stick out no matter where he is."

"It might surprise you how inconspicuous he can be."

As they drove toward the center of Loreto, Kevin looked out the window and tears began welling up in his eyes. Tyler noticed. "You okay, bruddah?"

"Sharon and I spent a weekend here right after we were married. She loved shopping at the local vendors' stalls on Salvatina. That's the tree-lined pedestrian street on the left. She thought the arbor it formed was a great example of people making the best of what they have. She always thought the best of everyone; even me. That's why I was so surprised she became a cop."

His sadness slowly turned to rage as he talked to Tyler. Noticing the change, Tyler placed a ham-sized hand on his shoulder. "We'll get those responsible. Don't let hate ruin the good she saw in you."

———————

Major Sandoval received a call. After listening for a few moments, he shut off the phone and directed the driver to go to Hotel La Mision, near the pier.

"Señors, this is your lucky day. We have rooms booked for you at La Mision. It would seem that your friends have purchased two vacant condominium buildings across the street from your hotel and are occupying them at the moment."

FIFTY FIVE

Harry discovered several new leads as to where his former partner, Tommy Thompson, may have hidden the laundered drug money everyone was searching for. Pondering this new information, he muttered aloud, "I need to go to Cabo and track down Tommy's contact."

While he was mentally formulating a plan, he recalled that his ex-wife had spent time with Tommy in Cabo. Just the thought of that slime-ball touching her made his skin crawl. After a moment of internal angst, his thoughts changed to how much he loved Dayna, and he reminded himself he needed to let the past stay in the past. "After all, she wasn't my wife at the time," he said, trying to find a way to accept what he knew would always be a contentious part of their relationship. He called her.

"Dayna? How would you like to spend a few days in Cabo with me?"

Following a brief silence, Dayna replied, "Hello to you, too, Harry. Why do you want to go to Cabo?"

"I found some information on Tommy's financial dealings. Someone in Cabo had to be an intermediary for him. Maybe we can find out who, if we spend some time down there."

"How long will we be gone?"

"Shouldn't take more than three days. I've got a pretty good idea where to look."

"You know I'm not comfortable with Cabo…."

Harry interrupted her mid-sentence, "That's all in the past, Dayna. Just let it go. I want you on hand because you were with Tommy and may recognize some of the people he met."

"Nice try, Harry. I know Tommy and I being together still bothers you. But if you won't talk about it ever again, I'll go with you."

"Deal. Now, how soon can you be ready?" You start packing and I'll arrange a flight for us this afternoon."

"That all depends. Will I need any formal clothes?"

"Perhaps a nice outfit to wear for dinner, and that cute pink bikini I like."

"Harry, I like the way you're thinking, but that bikini is about two sizes too small these days."

He chuckled at that. "Call me when you're ready and I'll pick you up."

———————

The light jet Harry chartered was quickly covering the eight hundred plus miles to Cabo. Dayna sat across a small table from him in a comfortable leather seat, listening to his plan for finding Tommy's contact. Harry had found credit card receipts for three spots that Tommy frequented several times on each of his visits to Cabo.

"I brought photos of Tommy. I'll show them around at these places. Maybe someone will recognize him and be willing to talk. I brought plenty of cash to stir their memory."

"Isn't that a long shot, Harry? It's been over a year since he was killed."

"If Tommy was paying someone to be his runner, he'll remember his source of income being cut off, and my guess is, he'll be very willing to talk for the right price."

"Well, it certainly won't hurt to try. How much money do you think Tommy hid?"

"Originally, I thought it several hundred million, but there may be a billion or more. If he was laundering funds for the Chinese and the Mexicans, the amount could be huge."

"So, if the money is in California banks as you think, why would a runner in Cabo be important?"

"He may know the names of others who are involved. If I can just get some link to a bank and the name of whoever made the deposits, we can get the feds to check accounts."

"I'm still confused. Why wouldn't the drug people have already tracked the runner down and recovered the money?"

"They think Arona has that information. That's why they're after him. Arona thinks his boss wants him eliminated so he can take the money for himself. As long as Arona is alive, his boss can't make a move on the money without the cartel and Chinese finding out."

"Now you have me worried. What if the bad guys find out we're looking for the money, too?"

"We should be fine. After all that happened in San Diego, they already know we're after the same thing. They have no reason to harm us unless we find the money before they do. And, besides, we aren't going to keep it. Once we turn it over to the feds, we're no longer of any interest to anyone."

Dayna moved close to Harry and grasped his arm, giving it a gentle squeeze. "I hope you're right, Harry. I hope you're right."

FIFTY SIX

Melvin and crew settled into their respective rooms, then met downstairs to begin their surveillance of the drug dealers. Major Sandoval was correct. Having their targets right across the street was convenient, but also precarious. They could be easily spotted if they weren't careful. Hopefully, Major Sandoval and his unit were trustworthy and had not already told the cartel and Chinese of their arrival.

"I don't think we should go out as a group. Tyler, you come with me and we'll check out the buildings next door. Forest, you and Kevin get with the hotel people; see if we can get one of the rooms facing the buildings across the street. You two can keep an eye on our friends from there."

Markham and Whitehill got the room

they wanted. They set up a spotting scope and camera on the two buildings across the street. The only activity they saw was Tyler and Melvin strolling around the block like a couple of tourists, talking and stopping to take an occasional photograph. A short time later, Melvin and Tyler returned to the hotel and joined Forest and Kevin in the surveillance room.

"Did you see anything while we were out? Melvin asked.

"Just you and Tyler acting like tourists," responded Markham.

Kevin added, "This doesn't feel right. They either know we're here, or they have nothing to hide. They're carrying around several million dollars and are being way too public."

"You may be right, Kevin," Melvin said. "In the meantime, we just keep an eye on them and wait for the right moment to nab Truong and the Mexican. Not much is going to happen until it gets dark, so let's lay out our options. I've got photos of all sides of the buildings. I'll map out all the entrances and exits and we can figure out our best plan of attack. It won't be easy with the buildings built the way they are. The open parking below will give us cover but the only way to the living area is by stairways. "

Tyler picked up the phone. Everyone turned and stared at him. "What? I'm hungry. I'm ordering room service. You guys want some food?"

"If you think it would be okay, there's a place just down the street called Koko Chang's that has great Chinese and Mexican food," said Kevin.

"Hold on. They're on the move," said Markham, who had been watching through the scope. "That must be Truong, and what appears to be four bodyguards, three Chinese and one Mexican."

The other three moved to the window. They watched as five men came out of the building and began walking toward the front of La Mision.

Melvin directed, "Kevin, you and Markham keep an eye on their building. Tyler, let's see where they're going."

Just moments after their targets passed, Tyler and Melvin exited La Mision, resumed their tourist act, and fell in some fifty yards behind the men. They headed down the street that fronted the marina, and appeared to be in no particular hurry. They had gone about a block when the group stopped, turned left, and entered a restaurant.

As Tyler and Melvin got closer, they saw the brightly colored building and sign declaring "KOKO CHANG fine Chinese and authentic Mexican food."

"Well, Tyler, looks like you get to eat after all. Let's see if the food is as good as Kevin says."

"Good idea. I'm starved."

"Let me call Forest and Kevin, then we'll go in."

FIFTY SEVEN

An older black Lincoln limousine and a uniformed chauffer met Harry and Dayna at the bottom of the stairs as they stepped off of the plane.

"Wow, Harry. I'm impressed!" Dayna declared.

"Thanks. You're worth it," responded Harry, having the good sense not to tell her it came with the charter.

As they entered the limo, Harry instructed the driver to take them to the Hacienda Beach Club near the marina where he had reserved a suite for three days.

"Are you trying to take advantage of me, Harry Walters? This place is beautiful."

"Oh, I hope so. But first things first. Let's unpack, then we can stroll over to Lazaro Cardenas Street and check out the restaurants we need to investigate."

Cardenas Street was just a short walk from the Hacienda Beach Club. Both Harry and Dayna enjoyed the local people and scenery along the way.

"Cabo always reminds me of Italy."

"How's that, Harry?"

"No matter how many tourists shuffle in and out, it retains its own quaint culture and personality."

"I never thought about it that way, but I guess you're right. I never really paid attention to anything other than what I was doing at the time."

They walked a bit further, dismissing several street vendors who beseeched them to stop for "just one Mexican minute" to see their wares. Suddenly, Harry did stop. "Well, I'll be damned!" he blurted.

"What?"

"The three places I'm looking for are all right here together. Sunny told me to Google the addresses before I left the office, but I ignored her. Better to be lucky than good, I guess."

"So, what are the restaurants?"

Pointing to each as he answered, Harry said, "The Hard Rock Café, La Trattoria, and over there, Squid Roe."

"That's quite a diverse trio from the looks of things."

"You want a beer?"

"Sure."

"Let's go see what the Hard Rock has to offer."

Even at mid-afternoon, the café was jumping with a young crowd of party people. "Must be a cruise ship in town. Looks like everyone came ashore for the cheap beer."

Removing several photos of Tommy Thompson from his coat, Harry started inquiring if any of the staff had ever seen him. One of the more endowed young waitresses said she knew him, but hadn't seen him in quite a while. "Like a year. Like, you know? He was, like, a lot of fun, big tipper."

"Did he ever come in with anyone else?"

"Oh yeah. Like, there was this redhead, you know? They always came in together and partied hearty, like, you know?"

"Can you tell me where I can find her?"

Acting as though she had suddenly had a massive stroke, she put her hand to her chin and mouth like in deep thought. "Well, like, it's been a long time, you know?"

Harry pulled a twenty from his wallet;

she snatched it quickly from his hand.

"She and this guy didn't show up for several months. Then she started coming in with an actor. Last I heard, she moved to Hollywood to be his nanny."

Harry took another twenty out. He held it with a firm grip as he handed the girl a pen and small notebook. "This is yours if you write down the name of the actor and the nanny."

Harry and Dayna left the Hard Rock without their beer, and moved to La Trattoria. As they entered, they were greeted by the hostess. "Table for two?"

"Not right now," Harry replied. "Could I please see a menu? We're looking for a place to have dinner."

"Certainly, Señor." Handing Harry their dinner menu, she waited while he perused the offerings and conferred with Dayna.

"Could you reserve a quiet table for two at seven-thirty tonight? Walters is my name."

"Of course, Señor Walters."

"A couple of other things before I leave. Would you chill two bottles of the Calixa Chardonnay and have them ready for our meal?" Then taking the photos out of his pocket, he showed them to the girl and asked if she had seen Thompson.

"No, señor, but I have only worked here a short while. Perhaps the dinner staff knows your friend."

"Perhaps. Muchas gracias."

"Prego," she replied, then giggled a bit. "I'm practicing my Italian."

"Buon giorno. Ci vediamo dopo."

"Buon giorno, signori."

"I still haven't had that beer you promised me," chided Dayna.

"I know. Let's go see what Squid Roe is all about."

They stood outside of Squid Roe, reading the signs, while a steady stream of revelers flowed in and out. The signs read, "Squid Roe, restaurant, bar, and a clothing line made with cotton and other stuff."

"That's as close as you're going to get to truth-in-advertising here in Mexico."

"Let's go in and get that beer."

Inside was all they expected, and more. Wall-to-wall people were encased in a pure Mexican cantina atmosphere. Everyone seemed just drunk enough to relax their inhibitions and make their visit to Squid Roe a memorable one. Dayna and Harry moved deeper into the door and were met by a vivacious waitress who inquired, "Party or food, folks?"

"Just a couple of beers for us. This is quite a place."

"Wait 'til the Hollywood folks start showing up. That's when this place really gets crazy."

"Does that happen often?"

"Every night about ten o'clock. Then it's full-out until three or four in the morning. Most of the tourists fade out before the celebrities do."

"Who do we have in town now?" Dayna asked, to Harry's surprise. She chuckled a bit when she saw the look on his face.

"We don't tell people in advance. Come in tonight and see for yourselves. Some of our regulars are over there on our 'Wall of Shame,' if you would like to see who might come in. What kind of beer do you want?"

"Do you have Bohemia?"

"You want the Obscura or the Lager?"

"One of each," Harry answered. Then, turning to Dayna, "Unless you want a Corona."

"The lager is fine."

While they were waiting for their

beer, they studied the photos on the "Wall of Shame." There were numerous musicians, movie stars and athletes who had frequented Squid Roe. Included in the collection was an odd photo of John Elway and his first wife, in a basically orange-colored picture with a large group of faces surrounding them in black and white. As Dayna studied the photo, she squinted and looked more closely, "Isn't that Tommy in the background, the one just to the right of Elway, with his arm around a young Mexican?"

"It sure is. Maybe the fellow he has his arm around is the one we're looking for."

Just then, the waitress appeared with a full tray of drinks. She sorted out the two beers for Harry and Dayna. "That'll be five dollars."

Harry handed her a fifty. "You can keep the change if you can tell me who this is in the photo," pointing to Thompson's drinking companion in the photo.

"Easiest tip I ever made. That's Manuel Ortega, one of our evening bartenders. The guy with him was a big spender from Santa Barbara… Tommy somebody. I read in the newspapers that his wife shot him about a year ago."

"Will Manuel be in tonight? I'd like

to talk to him."

"Yeah. In fact, his shift starts in about forty-five minutes if you want to wait for him. Why do you want to talk with Manuel?"

"I'm an attorney. I'm representing the 'Tommy somebody's' children. Before we can finish probate on his will, I have to clear up a claim that he had a couple of children with a Mexican girl here in Cabo. Perhaps Manuel can give me some more information on who Tommy hung around with"

"Oh sure. The way those two chased women, either one could have a bunch of little bastards running around."

"You're not Manuel's biggest fan, I take it?"

"He's everything that's bad. Only interested in money. He dated a friend of mine for a while and treated her like dog crap. He's a pig."

"What's your name?"

"Rose."

"Really?"

"Really. Rose Quintana."

"Well, Rose Quintana, here's another fifty. In return, I'd like you to give a message to Manuel. Have him come talk with me at my hotel. Can you do that?"

"Hell yes."

Taking out one of his business cards, he wrote, "Hacienda Beach Club" and the suite number on it, then told Rose that Manuel could call him on his cell phone so they could set up an appointment. "Tell him there's one hundred dollars in it for him."

Rose looked at the card and the fifty. "Thank you, Mr. Walters. I'll make sure he gets the message. Don't worry; for a hundred dollars, Manuel would strangle his own mother."

Harry and Dayna finished their beer, then headed back to the Hacienda.

"Why didn't you just wait and talk with Manuel at the restaurant?"

"If he buys my story about Tommy's children, he won't be as suspicious and there won't be as much distraction."

FIFTY EIGHT

"Wat you ting, brah? Is dis place da kine or wat?" Tyler questioned Melvin in his pidgin slang.

"Is nō ka ʻoi. Good Asian and Mexican food, all in one place."

Both were enjoying their meals and listening to the conversation at the table near them where Truong and his Mexican counterpart sat. The Mexican bodyguard sat by himself near the main door, while the two Chinese sat at a table near Truong. Melvin leaned toward Tyler and softly asked, "Can you hear what they are talking about?"

Tyler nodded and held his large hand up to quiet Melvin. After a few moments, he said, "They are talking about a shipment they are getting ready at their warehouse in Topolobampo. My Chinese is not as good as yours, but I think they said they are planning on sending in more people from Loreto to help oversee the distribution to each ship."

Tyler listened for another few minutes. "All of this is coming down in two days. They are waiting for El Jefe to show up so he and Truong can finalize the deal. Evidently, El Jefe will be here later today."

A waitress stopped at Melvin's and Tyler's table and asked if they wanted dessert. Tyler, with a big smile, responded, "You bet! What do you have?"

"Our Mexican special today is flan, with Mexican coffee, and our Chinese special is Gay Don Go."

"I love steamed sponge cake. Do you serve it hot?" asked Melvin.

"However you like, sir."

"Then I'll have the sponge cake."

Turning to Tyler, she asked, "And you, sir?"

"Do you have any fruit?"

"Mangoes, bananas, pineapple, coconut, strawberries and oranges. All from local growers."

"That sounds good. Bring me the coffee, flan, sponge cake, and a big bowl of mixed fruit," answered Tyler, holding his hands apart to indicate how large a bowl of fruit he wanted.

At that same time, Truong and the Mexican finished their meals and were leaving. They were quickly joined by their bodyguards and departed from the restaurant in unison.

———————

"Forest, our friends just left the restaurant and should be headed back your way. Leave Kevin in the room. You go down and keep an eye on them. Tyler and I will be there in about fifteen minutes. Tyler is having dessert."

"Dessert? We haven't had anything since breakfast."

"I know. We didn't forget you; we have a large sack of take-out for you and Kevin."

"I say, old chap, that's mighty kind of you."

"Get downstairs and see if our friends are headed to their building."

"Already there. And, yes, they're passing as we speak. We've got eyes on them, so you and Tyler hurry back."

FIFTY NINE

Dayna and Harry sat quietly, snuggled up on an overstuffed loveseat staring at the lush pool and grounds of the Hacienda Beach Club. Just beyond was the beach and the marina. Harry answered his chiming cell phone with, "Harry Walters."

"Mr. Walters, Rose Quintana gave me your card. I understand you want information regarding Tommy Thompson?"

"Are you Manuel Ortega?"

"Yes I am. Pardon my manners. I forgot to introduce myself. If it would be convenient, would you have time to talk now? I just dropped off an acquaintance at the Hacienda and am in the lobby."

"I'm in Suite 206. I'll be waiting."

"Thank you. I'll be right there."

Harry pressed the end call button on his cell phone and turned to Dayna. "You're in for a big surprise. Manuel Ortega is on his way here. He just called from the lobby."

Dayna gathered up the bottle of wine and glasses. She took them to the wet bar, then headed straight to the bathroom to "put her face on."

The doorbell rang; Harry checked the peep hole. Outside his door was a hotel clerk and a young Mexican man Harry presumed was Manuel Ortega. When Harry opened the door, the clerk said, "This is Mr. Ortega. Do you have an appointment with him, Mr. Walters?"

"Yes. I do." Motioning Ortega in, he thanked the clerk. "I appreciate your bringing him up."

"You're welcome, Mr. Walters. Our guests' security is our primary goal. If it's not too much of an inconvenience, could you please inform us of any visitors in advance?"

"Certainly. Thank you, again."

Shutting the door, he mumbled, "Must not have read the house rules. Mr. Ortega, please have a seat. I have several questions about Tommy Thompson's activities here in Cabo. I represent Mr. Thompson's children, and I'm trying to complete the probate of his will so his children can begin receiving their inheritance. What I am most concerned about is whether or not Mr. Thompson may have fathered any children here in Mexico. Can you tell me anything about Mr. Thompson's, shall we say, extracurricular activities?"

"Perhaps, Mr. Walters. Rose said you were offering one hundred dollars for information. Is that true?"

"Oh, yes it is. I'm sorry. I forgot to mention that small detail."

"No small detail to me, Mr. Walters. I'm trying to pay my way through school."

"I'm familiar with your plight. I worked my way through law school. If you have verifiable information useful to me, I'm sure I can sweeten the pot. By the way, what are you studying?"

"International Relations at Berkeley. I work here summers and break times."

"I must say, your English and deportment are excellent. How many languages do you speak?"

"Four fluently, at the moment. My goal is to reach six by graduation."

"Quite impressive! I had trouble learning what little Italian and Spanish I speak."

"Da vero."

"Amen to that. So tell me, how did you and Mr. Thompson meet?"

"He came into Squid Roe one night

with some buxom second-string actress and was throwing a lot of money around to get attention. I made a point of sucking up to him to ensure I got a big tip. His actress friend got drunk and started hitting on me. I was afraid she would screw up my chance of a big tip, so I pretended not to notice. Thompson called me over to his table and asked if I knew where we could get some real women. He gave me five hundred dollars. We left the Squid and his drunk actress to go to a high-class party at the 'Dorado.' We spent the rest of the night with two young housewives from La Jolla. The next night, he shows up at the Squid alone. Again, he asked if I knew of any more parties we could go to. I told him I could hook him up, but I couldn't join him because I had to work. He said I could work for him; he offered me a thousand dollars a week and said I could keep working at the Squid."

"What sort of work did you do for him?"

"Mostly running errands. He had a lot of real estate deals here in Mexico, and he had me carry everything from money to contracts to the buyers and sellers."

Harry, not wanting to sound too eager about what Ortega was telling him, recentered the conversation. "I see. What about women?"

"Any time I spotted someone I thought he would like, I would set them up. Some were one-night stands, others he might play around with for several weeks."

"That brings me to my most important question. Do you think he may have fathered children with any of these women?"

"No way. He was always bragging about his vasectomy. He said it was the best thing his wife ever made him do."

"Would you be willing to sign an affidavit regarding what you what you just told me?"

"Sure, why not? He's dead, and I sure don't have anything to hide."

"Rose doesn't seem to be a big fan of yours."

"I'm sure she isn't. The day after we were engaged, she caught me with her best friend. Unfortunately, her friend got pregnant and had an abortion. So you can see why neither of them thinks much of me. My regret is that I didn't know about the pregnancy until after the abortion. I had a vasectomy the day after I found out about the abortion. So you see, Tommy and I had stories to share."

"Thank you for your candor, Manuel. Would you like some wine or coffee?"

"Some wine would be nice."

Pouring them each a glass of wine, Harry continued the questioning. "I really appreciate you providing me with this information. You mentioned you ran a lot of errands for Tommy?"

"He said he didn't trust banks. He had me deliver cash for real estate closings; he also had me pick up cash bags from real estate brokers here in Mexico and take them to brokers in California."

"You carried large amounts of cash across the border?"

"I worried at first that it might be illegal, but I was never stopped or questioned. I was always given specific directions on the exact day, time and border station to use. I figured he was avoiding taxes, and if I was ever caught, I would just tell the authorities everything I knew."

"Well that may have gotten you less jail time, but I'm glad you never had to find out."

"When Thompson got shot, it scared the hell out of me. I played it close to the vest for several months. I didn't even hang around with any of his friends afterward."

"Perhaps Tommy skimmed some money from his real estate deals. If he did, that money could go to his kids. Can you give me the names of banks and people you delivered to so I can check them out?"

"Can I get in trouble if he was stealing and having me transport the money?"

"Well, Tommy sure can't testify against you. All I want is for his kids to get what's coming to them. Their dad was killed by their mother, and she'll be in jail for the rest of her life. The more money these kids can get, the better off they'll be. Their guardians will see to that. All I need is the affidavit about Tommy's vasectomy. No one has to know about the money."

"You've got a deal."

Harry pulled out his wallet, counted out ten hundred dollar bills, and handed them to Manuel. "Here you go. This should buy a few books."

Harry walked over to the suite's desk and picked up the scratch pad and pen. He handed them to Manuel. "Please write down the names of all the businesses, banks, and anyone else that you made deliveries to, or pick-ups from. Any information that might help me get Thompson's children their just inheritance." Harry sat patiently, sipping his glass of wine, until Manuel finished writing.

"Here you are, Mr. Walters. Good hunting. That's all I can remember right now. If I think of anything else, I'll call you at the number on your card."

"Vaya con Dios, mi amigo."

"That's very kind, Mr. Walters. Thank you."

When Ortega left, Dayna came out of the bedroom and gave Harry a big hug. "You are something else, Harry Walters! What a performance! But, weren't you worried he would know the Feds would confiscate the money?"

"I guess my courtroom experience helped me determine he was nice, but not too sharp. He was mostly interested in making money. I was a bit surprised at his sincerity when it came to helping the children, though. That abortion really affected him."

SIXTY

The bright orange sun was slowly sinking into the Sea of Cortez. Tourists and locals alike stopped for a few moments to take in the amazing sunset. As darkness settled in, Melvin and crew became more vigilant. If what they heard in the restaurant was true, El Jefe could arrive at any time. Tyler was finishing the last few scraps of a room-service meal when Kevin called out, "He's here."

A large, gray SUV pulled up to the building and turned in to the parking alcove on the east side, facing the window where Melvin and his men were now intently watching. Two large goons with automatic rifles got out of the vehicle and carefully checked their surroundings. One of them motioned to the SUV. A third man got out and stood guard while a well-dressed man got out and walked quickly to the building's entrance. Once the well-dressed man and the guard were safely inside the building, the two goons and the driver got back into the SUV and sped away.

"Looks like El Jefe has arrived," said Melvin. "Do you recognize him, Kevin?"

"Not from this distance in the dark. I'll get the photos we just took downloaded into the computer and take a nice close look at his face."

"Send the digital photos to our FBI contacts. Maybe they can ID him through facial recognition. While Kevin is doing that, the rest of us need to get ready for our assault."

During the next few minutes, Melvin and the others donned body armor and checked all the weaponry the navy had provided.

"Any luck on the ID?"

"No. I've not seen him before. He doesn't look Mexican, but, looks can be deceiving."

"You should know. Get your gear on and let's go get up-close and personal."

The men slipped unnoticed out of a door at the back of the hotel into a small alley filled with dumpsters and trash. Across the street, the same alley afforded more dumpsters and cover. The men ran quickly across the alley and reached the ground-floor parking for the condo. They climbed the stairs to the second floor living space.

Melvin checked the area for cameras and guards, but surprisingly, none were found. Once inside, they braced for a gun battle, but still no activity. They were standing in a dimly lit hallway that had large bedrooms on each side. Melvin motioned everyone to move forward. As they approached the main room at the end of the hall, they heard voices. Melvin stopped for a moment, listening, then told his men, "They're dividing the drugs and discussing the best way to get the stuff into the States."

Crouching low, Melvin inched out of the hallway and headed toward the voices. To his right was a large living room area and an open-concept kitchen with a dining counter in between. He could see El Jefe and Truong at the counter, going over a map and talking delivery details. Flanking them were seven guards. Four were seated at the dining table eating. One guard was near Melvin on the right, another on the opposite side of the room and the third at the front entrance.

Markham signaled Melvin and called his attention to an electrical breaker box on the wall near him. He made hand gestures like he was shutting the power off and motioned for Melvin's approval. Melvin held up his hand signaling for Markham to wait. He then directed each of the other men on which section he should attack. That done, he gave Markham the go signal.

As soon as the power went off, Melvin and company charged into the main room. Unfortunately, a few seconds later, the emergency lighting in the room came on and one of the guards started shooting. When all of the shooting stopped, Melvin surveyed the room. Five of the seven guards were dead, but somehow, in all of the gunfire, El Jefe and Truong managed to escape. Tyler was slumped against a wall. Melvin saw blood on him and hurried over to his friend.

"Tyler! Are you hit?"

"Yeah, boss. Ten times, if I count right."

Melvin stared incredulously at Tyler, who was sitting there like a fascinated kid with a new toy, picking spent slugs from his body armor and counting them.

"Tyler, you're bleeding. Where are you hit?"

"Oh, that. Just my leg. It's okay. Through and through. Didn't hit anything important."

Tyler resumed his preoccupation with the slugs and Melvin hurried over to Kevin who was lying on the floor bleeding from the right side of his neck. A bullet had grazed his neck just above the shoulder. Melvin grabbed a towel from the kitchen and placed it on the wound. As he was checking for additional wounds, Kevin came to, blinking his eyes.

"Did we get El Jefe?"

"No. He and Truong got away. Go help Tyler with his leg. I need to find Forest."

Searching the entire compound, Melvin couldn't find Markham or any sign of El Jefe or Truong. The SUV was also missing. Melvin returned to the kitchen where Kevin was attempting to bandage Tyler's leg.

"Hold still, you big oaf. I need to clean this out before we bandage it."

"Can't help it. It tickles."

"Tickles? My God, man! You're something else. I'm glad you're on our side."

"I couldn't find Markham or our targets. He must have gone after them when they left."

"He's got a satellite phone. He'll probably give us a call in a little while saying he's got Truong and wants us to pick him up."

"I appreciate your optimism, Kevin.

Let's hope you're right. Speaking of phones, I'd best call Major Sandoval and ask him to collect the bodies."

SIXTY ONE

Thank you, gentlemen," said Major Sandoval to Melvin, Tyler and Kevin, who were all seated around a conference table in Sandoval's office. "We have been after Truong and his Mexican counterpart for two years. And even though we don't have them in custody, we have enough information from the computer they left at the condo to seriously disrupt their operation. There will be a full-scale military assault on their Guaymas and Topolobampo distribution sites tomorrow. That will, at least, slow them down for several months and cut off their cash flow."

"Have you identified El Jefe, yet?" asked Kevin.

"No, sir. But your photos are most intriguing. He doesn't appear to be Mexican. Our facial experts speculate he may be Russian, which opens up a whole new can of worms. Maybe your FBI will be able to identify him."

"Do you need anything further from us?" asked Melvin.

"No, Colonel Momi. I've assigned a car and driver to you. Just let him know when you're ready and he can take you to the airport."

"The airport? Are you trying to get rid of us?"

"As a matter of fact, yes. So far, no one knows we let Americanos come into Loreto. The sooner you leave, the better. Rest assured we will make every attempt to find your friend and apprehend the drug lords."

"Again, my thanks, Major Sandoval. We should be ready before sunrise."

"Are we just going to leave Markham here on his own?" Kevin asked when they arrived back at the hotel.

"No. I've already called two of my associates from Honolulu to fly here and continue the search. They should be here sometime this afternoon. I've given them a full report, including a description of the SUV. Now, I need to call Harry and tell him what's happened."

SIXTY TWO

Markham was pleased that there wasn't much traffic on the road. There was just enough moonlight for him to see his desolate surroundings. He pushed a little harder on the gas pedal and said to himself, "Gotcha now, you buggers," as he spotted a vehicle a quarter of a mile or so in front of him.

He eased off the gas when he confirmed it was the SUV he was after and followed at a reasonable distance as the SUV entered the small village of Santa Rosalia. The SUV took a direct line to the ferry boat dock and parked in the parking lot.

Markham stopped and watched as the trio went to the ticket window to purchase a vehicle permit, then returned to the SUV and moved it into the loading area. Markham shut his vehicle off by disconnecting the wires he had pulled from under the dash and left it parked on the street. "The owner will be happy I didn't destroy their car, unless someone else steals it before the police spot it."

He made his way to the passenger ticket terminal, contemplating how he could get on the ferry and still remain undetected. He spotted El Jefe, Truong and a Chinese bodyguard carrying two metal briefcases coming toward him. Markham stepped out of line and watched from behind a kiosk as the men got closer. When the three were near enough for him to clearly see their faces, he was surprised to see a face he recognized. "Sergei Obelensky," he uttered out loud. A thousand thoughts rushed through his mind. Obelensky was tied in with the Russian mob when he first ran into him in Ensenada several years ago.

Putting two and two together, he concluded that Obelensky was now El Jefe, the head of the Mexican cartel everyone was looking for. Thinking aloud, he said, "That explains why no one has been able to find any Mexican connection. Obelensky probably killed Ochoa and assumed control. El Jefe is a damned Ruskie! It also explains why my wife and Kevin's wife were murdered. I've always thought it odd that the Mexicans would kill them as a warning. They generally kidnap people and collect ransom rather than commit singular murders. When they want to scare people into silence, they kill people in large numbers and make it public. The Russians, on the other hand, prefer a quieter, more subtle method."

As Markham recalled the death of his wife, many years' of anger began to well up. He knew he needed to kill Obelensky.

He surveyed the crowd around him; he began thinking how and when would be the best place to shoot all three. Then he remembered he may need to keep El Jefe alive to help Kevin prove his innocence. To his surprise, the three men walked quickly past the line of waiting people toward the parking lot. He followed and watched as they were picked up by another SUV and a new driver. After the three got in the vehicle, it made a U-turn and sped off in the direction of Loreto.

Fortunately for Forest, his SUV was still right where he had left it. He jumped in, did his trick with the wires to start it, and resumed his chase.

SIXTY THREE

"My name is Walters. I have a reservation for two at seven thirty."

"Thank you, Señor Walters," said the hostess as she checked her reservations book. "Right this way."

She led them to a quiet corner table at the back of the dining room. After they were seated, she said, "Your waiter, Antonio, will be here with your chilled wine in just a moment."

"Good evening, Mr. Walters, and also to your lovely lady. I'm Antonio, at your service. You ordered the Calixa Chardonnay?"

"Yes, indeed."

"Do you wish it opened now or when your food arrives?"

"A glass now would be fine."

Antonio deftly handed menus to Harry and Dayna, then opened the wine. He handed the cork to Harry for inspection, and when Harry set it on the table, he poured a small amount into a sommelier's cup and tasted it. Nodding his approval, he poured a small amount into Harry's glass for his tasting. Harry sipped from the glass; declared it a bit tanniny, but acceptable for seafood. Antonio poured two glasses, then left them to look over the menu.

"The seafood linguine looks good to me," said Dayna.

"I'm going to try the Saltimbocca Caprese. That's just a strange enough combination to be either really good or awful."

After a series of delightful appetizers, Harry and Dayna began the tasting and appraisal of their entrée choices.

"This linguine is fresh; handmade. And the seafood is absolutely delicious. How is your Saltimbocca?"

"Other than a little too much olive oil, mine is a very good combination. A few capers would really help."

"Oh, Harry. You and your food."

As Antonio was clearing the entrée plates and presenting them with dessert menus, Harry's phone rang. "It's Melvin," he declared to Dayna. "Hello, Melvin. Everything okay at your end?"

Harry sat quietly listening for the next few minutes while Melvin reported on the raid of the drug compound and the end result. When Melvin finished, Harry asked, "Do you need anything from me?"

"No. We'll meet you back in San Diego. When are you going back?"

"Tomorrow morning. I'll be in my office at two o'clock. See you then."

Harry gave a synopsis of Melvin's news to Dayna, then the two of them ordered dessert.

———

Back in their room at the resort, Dayna and Harry sat in bed propped up by large, fluffy, cozy pillows. "That was a lovely meal, Harry. Thank you," Dayna said, as she placed her head on his shoulder. Harry started talking about everything he needed to do when they got back to San Diego. When Dayna didn't respond, he looked down at her and found that she was sound asleep. He gently moved her from his shoulder, rearranged her pillow, and pulled the covers up to her chin.

SIXTY FOUR

Markham didn't have any problem catching up with the El Jefe and Truong vehicle. There were very few cars on the road this late at night.

As they approached Loreto, Markham kept a keen eye on the target. The drug kingpins turned right at the first intersection, then continued to the edge of town. They stopped at a small abandoned house.

As the four men entered the building by a side door, Markham parked and carefully approached the house on foot. There was just enough moonlight for him to note his surroundings. A large clump of bougainvillea provided a screen to his approach, and he was able to get within ten feet of the house. In front of him was a boarded-up window. The door through which the men had entered was just around the corner on the right.

Markham waited several minutes,

making sure he hadn't been seen, before inching toward the house. As he got closer, he could hear two men talking in broken English, discussing how they were going to get out of Mexico and what to do with the package. Markham assumed the "package" to be the drugs and the cash they escaped with when all the shooting broke out.

Another voice, with a definite Mexican accent, said, "I finally got Torres out of bed. He says he can have twenty more men here first thing in the morning, if you want."

"If whoever ambushed us is still nosing around, that may not be a good idea. For now, tell him to bring us another vehicle– a sedan–so we can go to La Paz."

Speaking into his cell phone, the Mexican returned to that conversation. "Torres, El Jefe says he needs you to bring a sedan…No. Just you. And bring some more ammo…Si. Adios.

"He'll be here before seven o'clock," he reported to the men in the room, after disconnecting his call.

The next voice Markham heard was speaking Chinese. Markham wasn't exactly fluent in Mandarin, but understood enough to know Truong was directing his bodyguard to set up a sentry post outside. Markham moved to some smaller shrubs at the side of the house. He was able to see inside when the bodyguard came out, followed by the Mexican bodyguard. Inside the house, there was just one big room that held a table in the center with several chairs on either side. Sergei and Truong were seated; four cases sat on the table. As the door of the house closed, Markham quickly returned to his hiding spot behind the bougainvillea. "Are these pretty flowers for my funeral, God? Or theirs?" he quietly uttered.

The two guards talked for a few moments, then the Mexican started walking toward the rear of the building. The Chinese guard moved by the door to keep watch on the front of the house.

Markham hurried to the side of the house which was hidden by dense vegetation, and waited for the Mexican to come to him. The guard was not aware of Markham until a hand suddenly clamped over his mouth and Markham inserted a knife into his back. The guard went limp and Markham pulled him into the vegetation.

Markham then returned to his observation post by the bougainvillea and saw that the Chinese guard had not moved. Using one of the oldest tricks in the book,

Markham pick up a large rock and tossed it into a trash pile beside the house. The Chinese guard immediately went to investigate and Markham dispatched him in the same manner as the Mexican.

Markham picked up the Chinese guard's automatic weapon and walked to the front door. He calmly opened the door and pointed the weapon at Truong and El Jefe. "Evening, gents. Please be kind enough to place your hands behind your heads and don't move." As he neared the table where the two drug lords were sitting, El Jefe made a sudden move toward a pistol lying on the table. Markham leaned forward and struck him just above the left eye with the barrel of his weapon and he fell to the floor.

After tying both men's hands securely behind their backs, he picked up two metal cases from the table and said, "Let's go for a walk chaps. I need to get you back to the U.S. of A."

SIXTY FIVE

Honey Boy and Mei Li flew into Cabo San Lucas where they immediately rented a car. As they drove Avenida Leon Vacario into town, Honey Boy turned to Mei Li. "I thought Cabo was supposed to be a swank place, where all the movie stars and rich people hang out. Is there something about this place I'm not seeing?"

"All the luxury and money is down by the water. It's typical of most Mexican resort towns. The big hotels, shopping areas and bars are all around the marina. But, you're right. The recent economy slump sure hasn't done much to improve the living conditions for the locals. Do you notice the similarity to Hawaii?"

"Turn left on Coco Palmso," the sweet voice on the car's GPS intoned. Another series of directional prompts which led them through several short left and right turns brought Honey Boy and Mei Li to Mexico

Nineteen. From there, it was just a few minutes' drive, even in heavy traffic, to Mexico One and the Transpeninsular Highway.

Honey Boy fiddled with the radio until he found some "ranchero" music he liked. He set the cruise control to just under the speed limit. The last thing they needed was any attention from the Mexican police. Mei Li settled back for the five-hour drive to Loreto and began studying several maps she had obtained from the rental car agency.

"You know, since GPS navigation is so easy to get by phone or in cars nowadays, they quit giving out decent paper maps. This map barely lists the main roads and towns."

"So use your satellite phone. What are you looking for?"

"All of the roads and access routes from Loreto. We have no idea which direction Markham and the druggies may have taken. When you're in a hurry, the old 'shortest distance between two points' is usually what people choose. I guess I'll have to Google the area to get the information I need."

"Having trouble catching up with all the new technology?"

"No," Mei Li shot back. "It's just a lot

easier for me to spot patterns and topographical barriers on a regular paper map."

"Did you check the glove compartment or console? Maybe there's a better map in there."

Mei Li opened the console. The only thing to be found was an old chewing gum package. When she opened the glove compartment, to her delight, there was a National Geographic map of the Baja Peninsula and a AAA Road Guide.

"Just what I needed. Nice guess."

"Guess, nothing. I'm just better at this than you," he said flippantly.

"It's going to be a long five hours to Loreto if you don't lose that attitude."

"Pull your horns in. We've got a lot to prepare for before we get to Loreto. These drug guys know the area like the back of their hands, and so does Markham. The way I see it, they have three ways to get out of Loreto. The airport, the marina, and by car. Do those maps give you a good picture of the easiest way out from where the shoot-out occurred?"

"The marina is just down the street. They wouldn't have needed the SUV to get there unless there was something in it they needed. We ought to check if the SUV was left at the marina or the airport. That will narrow down the options."

"Make a note to see if there is a ferry boat that carries vehicles out of Loreto."

"No, but according to the 'Geographic,' there's a terminal at Santa Rosalia which is a couple hours north. The ferry goes from there to Los Mochis on the mainland. La Paz, to the south of us, has a terminal at Pichilingue that goes to Topolobampo and Matzatlán. Both runs are long overnight trips according to this. We'll have to check the schedule to see which their most likely choice was."

"Call Melvin and see if he can get us a current timetable."

Mei Li dialed Melvin's number and waited until the voicemail chimed.

"Hey, Boss, this is Mei Li. We need a time frame on your party last night and a current ferry boat departure schedule. Call me back. We're about three hours out of Loreto."

After closing the call, she turned to Honey Boy and said, "Must be busy. Where do you want to start when we get there?"

We can check into the La Mision Hotel. We'll ask folks in the area if they saw or heard anything. Speaking of checking in, does Tyler know you're down here posing as my wife?"

"I'm sure he knows by now. Why?"

"Why?! I don't want to get on his bad side. He's awfully protective of you."

"I can take care of myself. He's the only man I ever met that I couldn't get the best of."

"Excuse me?"

With a giggle, Mei Li replied, "And you. You two are the exception, but I don't think I'll run into too many giant Tongans or Samoans down here in Mexico. I thought we were chasing a Chinaman."

"Okay, but don't get upset if I make an extra effort to keep you safe."

"How much trouble can we get into? We're just looking for a friend."

"Along with the Chinese and Mexican drug cartels. Did Melvin say anything about weapons?"

"There are two pistols and some ammunition in a safety deposit box at the Mision Hotel. Melvin gave me the security code and password. He also gave me a Major Sandoval's phone number if we need serious backup. Sandoval is Mexican army, and, according to Melvin, a good man."

"That'll help. What about cash?"

"Melvin said for me to just use my

credit card and use ATMs to get what we need. I brought three hundred dollars with me. Do you have any cash?"

"About a hundred twenty dollars. A few hundred more should be enough to buy any information we need."

"Any ideas as to why Markham hasn't called anyone?"

"He has a bad habit of going dark when he's after someone. Harry told me that he doesn't hear from him for weeks at a time, and then, poof, he just shows up like nothing happened."

"I'll send him texts just the same. Sooner or later, he'll get tired of me pestering him and call back."

"I wouldn't do that if I were you. He may have lost his phone. Or it could have been taken away from him. We don't want the wrong people to know who you are, and that we're out looking for him."

"Guess I'm a little rusty. That's what staying home does to a fearsome killer-for-hire."

SIXTY SIX

Melvin, Kevin and Tyler met Harry in his office and debriefed their adventures.

"While your associates and the Mexican army search for Markham, let's see what we can find from this list I got from Ortega," said Harry. "By the way, who did you send over from Honolulu?"

Melvin glanced at Tyler and replied, "Honey Boy and the Chinaman."

"You called Mei Li without asking me?" exploded Tyler.

"You would have said no. Relax, Tyler. She'll be fine with Honey Boy, and they can pass as a couple while they search for Markham."

"That's supposed to make me feel better?"

"You agreed to let her pick which jobs she wants to work. Remember?"

"We need a new agreement when this is over."

Harry spoke up in an effort to clear the air. "Let's break this list up and see if we can find any patterns."

For the next several hours, they pored over all the information they could get. As expected, a pattern became evident, and Harry began deciphering the locations and schedule of Tommy's money transfers.

"This is it, gentlemen. We have twenty banks in California, and four in Mexico, that were receiving money from Tommy twice a week. This is a lot bigger than I ever imagined! If each transfer was a half million, we're talking one-and-a-quarter billion dollars. Add that to the money at Ora Vista development, which Thompson was using as the main facade to launder the drug money, we could be at two billion dollars or more.

"That is far more than I anticipated," Harry continued. "From these numbers, it looks like Tommy was skimming about ten percent. He offset his cut with the interest on all the accounts, then added back in all the profit from the real estate deals."

Melvin tilted his head, "That explains why the cartel never caught on to his scheme. He was stealing their money and still making the cartel a profit. How did you figure out what he was doing?"

"About a month before we dissolved our partnership, Tommy and a shady banker set up a refunding on a large development. One day, they came back from a celebratory luncheon and Tommy started bragging that he was going to make one hundred thousand dollars–tax free–on the deal. When I asked him how, he tapped his temple with his index finger and said, 'Brains, my boy, brains. The profit I make on this deal will easily offset any extra fees that may be involved.' Then he winked at me and patted me on the back. That was the moment I decided I no longer wanted to be his partner. When I came back from Santa Barbara, I remembered him saying that, and began looking through his files again.

"There are a lot of people who are going to be arrested. I bet every one of the banks failed to file an SAR on Tommy's transfers. Most likely, they also failed to notify anyone of wires to foreign countries."

With a quizzical look on his face, Tyler asked, "What's an SAR?"

"Suspicious Activities Report. All banks are supposed to file one for any transaction of ten thousand dollars or more, or for less if there are questionable circumstances. That's why more and more money-laundering is being done through credit unions. They don't have the same reporting climate as banks."

"Wait until the FBI and DEA hear about this!" exclaimed Kevin.

"What? You don't think we should keep it for ourselves?" teased Melvin.

Harry looked intently at Melvin. "Good point, Melvin. Why shouldn't we get a piece of the pie? The Mexican army would be elated to get one sixth of a billion or two, and dear old Uncle Sam could certainly afford a small finder's fee if we lead them to the money."

"How small?" Tyler asked.

"Oh, no less than ten percent. Maybe as much as twenty percent."

"So we could each make four or five million dollars?"

"Your math and decimal point are both off a bit, Tyler. Nevertheless, I'll see if I'm able to sweet-talk the Feds into a deal for the information."

"Well then, Counselor, I think you should start practicing your sales pitch," said Kevin.

After the giddiness of speculation on how they would each spend their yet-to-bebargained new-found fortune, Melvin said, "We still have some unfinished business, gentlemen. What do we do about Markham?"

Harry replied, "Let's give Honey Boy and Mei Li a little more time. If they haven't found him by then, we get in touch with Sandoval and go back to Mexico. Get some rest, I'll start my little dance with the government."

SIXTY
SEVEN

Major Sandoval and his men cordoned off the condo complex where the shoot-out had taken place. Two Mexican federal police and the Loreto chief of police were onsite conducting a forensic investigation under the watchful eye of Major Sandoval. One of the Federales approached Sandoval. "Looks like an ambush to me. What do you think?"

"It's either that, or a drug deal that turned out differently than planned."

"We found a large pile of cocaine that looks uncut on the table and a trail of dust leading to the door. We also have blood samples from two areas where there were no bodies. Whoever killed these men may have been wounded. As soon as I get the results, I'll call you from Mexico City."

The Federale returned to his work. Sandoval strolled to the hallway. He took out his cell phone and dialed one of his trusted lieutenants, who was posted downstairs, and quietly asked, "Did you check every medical facility on the Baja to see if anyone has been treated for a gunshot wound?"

"Yes sir, Major."

Sandoval walked back into the room and asked the investigators for an estimate of how many people were involved.

"From the bullet holes and shell casings we found, I estimate ten to twelve people," replied the other Federale, who was busy taking photos and bagging evidence.

"Any ID on our dead men?"

"Nothing. We'll have to do the usual photo, dental and fingerprint search. Whoever they are, they have expensive clothing and don't have any of the usual drug tats or markings."

"Most likely, they're bodyguards for someone important."

"Right, Major. One other oddity—we have three different shell casings."

"Only three guns were used?"

"No. There were several. But some of the casings are European-made, and the others American- and Chinese-made. The European casings appear to be from small automatic weapons. The American casings are from .45 automatic pistols, and the

Chinese are 5.8 millimeter."

"Well that complicates matters. We haven't had Chinese involvement for several years. Maybe this is a new fight for territory."

After the bodies were hauled off and the building sealed, the Federales departed, and the police chief resumed his normal duties.

Sandoval walked toward his vehicle, pleased that he was able to get Melvin and his men out of the area without detection. As soon as he returned to the office, he called his FBI contact in San Diego to alert him to the blood and fingerprint samples that were being sent in. The agent agreed to respond with a "No Match Found in System" reply for Melvin and his crew.

Following a light rap on the door, the lieutenant entered the major's office. "We have a body down by the marina. The chief of police just called me. He said the man is Chinese and was shot twice. Once in the abdomen and once between the eyes."

"Get down there and see if anyone left by boat last night. Sounds like his friends decided to cut and run without him. Get our forensic people down there to see if they can identify the bullets. I specifically need to know if they're European, Chinese, or

American."

SIXTY EIGHT

"Sunny, will you get Agent Davis of the FBI on the line for me?"

A few moments later, Sunny rang Harry's intercom. "Agent Davis is on the line."

"Thank you, Sunny. Agent Davis. How would you like to get credit for one of the largest drug busts in California history?"

"You found the drug supply?"

"Some of it. But, more importantly, I think I know where all the money is."

"You figured out how Thompson was laundering the money?"

Harry picked up on the excitement in Davis' voice, so waited a moment before dropping the sales pitch.

"Perhaps. But first, I have a question. Is the government still giving rewards for information leading to drug arrests?"

"You old dog. What are you trying to pull off?"

"Well, since my people and I have spent the last couple of years trying to break this case open and several of us nearly lost our lives in the process, I think it would be nice if our government provided us with a nice retirement package. Surely a twenty percent finder's fee would be reasonable for breaking up a major drug cartel in Hawaii, Mexico and California, and recovering a substantial amount of cash from the money-laundering scheme that financed it all."

"How substantial?"

"Think about it, Davis. Very substantial."

"I'll have to run this by the Attorney General. He may want to play hardball and just arrest you for obstruction of justice."

"You know, memory lapse in us older people is a terrible thing. I sure hope I don't forget where I put all of the information."

"Point made. I'll call you back."

"Thank you, Agent Davis. I look forward to our next conversation."

SIXTY NINE

After the latest incident in Loreto, Melvin assembled everyone in Harry's office and brought them up to speed. "Sandoval said their sweep didn't turn up any more bodies or clues. He's headed to Topolobampo to clean up the distribution center."

"Do you want to go back down and see if you can find him?" Harry asked, concern in his voice.

"I'm not sure. My best guess is that he is still after Truong and El Jefe. No one knows the Baja better than Markham. I don't think we'll find him until he wants to be found."

Harry nodded. "I can update you on my conversations with the Attorney General about recovering all of the laundered money Tommy was squirreling away. He hasn't yet agreed to a finder's fee, but he hasn't said no. He said he needs a show of good faith that I'll turn all of the money over. I've stressed several times that we don't have the money. We just know where to find it."

"So now what happens?" asked Melvin.

"I'll set up a meeting with the Attorney General and show them what we have. I'm pushing for a twenty percent finder's fee, but even one percent will make us all rich."

"Good," said Tyler. "I've been looking forward to being a millionaire!"

"Harry, I've changed my mind. I think Kevin and I ought to go back to Mexico and hunt for Forest. I'll leave Tyler here to help as needed. Can you afford to keep us on the payroll a few more days?"

"Why not, Melvin? I'm going to be a millionaire soon," replied Harry, trying to bring a little levity to the situation. What are the chances he's still alive?"

"Considering we haven't been told he's dead, I would say pretty good."

SEVENTY

"Wow. This place is beautiful," exclaimed Mei Lie, as she and Honey Boy pulled up to the La Mision Hotel.

"If you say so. I'm not much of a fan of tourist hotels."

"Are you grumpy from our drive?" asked Mei Li as she slugged him on the shoulder.

"Let's get checked in and down to work."

"Fine, spoil sport."

As they were checking in, Mei Li inquired about the safety deposit box and the clerk dutifully took her to the secure area. On one wall was a series of electronic wall safes. After entering the security code and password, she opened the safe and withdrew a taped box. She joined Honey Boy back at the reception desk.

"Oh, I see your friend found your purse. Nice of her to leave it here on her way back to California."

"Her note says we have to pay for the safe rental. How much is it?"

"Only five dollars American, señora.

"Pay the man, dear."

"Try not to forget anything this time, please. You are starting to get expensive."

The clerk and surrounding guests were getting a chuckle out of the marital repartee and also from the fact that they were an odd couple. He stood well over six feet tall and weighed at least 300 pounds while she was barely over five feet and weighed one hundred pounds, tops.

"While you were getting your purse, the desk clerk told me there was a big gun battle across the street."

"Oh, my God! Is it safe to stay here?"

"Oh, si, señora. Just some drug people shooting each other. No tourists were harmed."

"Maybe we should go somewhere else."

"I assure you, you are safe, señora. The army and Federales are here. No harm will come to you."

"So, big fella, which bed do you want?"

"The one closest to the door, so I can protect you from anyone who might break in."

"Okay, big brother. What else did you learn from the desk clerk?"

"He said six people were killed in the shootout. They found a Chinese man shot to death down by the marina. At least that gives us an initial direction."

"Let's get down there and see if we can spot the SUV. If they took a boat, they could be anywhere."

———

Honey Boy didn't have to pay for information on the man who was shot. Everyone who worked or was near there was talking about a Chinese man being found next to some trash cans. Some said he had been shot many times. Others, just a few. But they all agreed he had been shot between the eyes. "I don't think Markham shot him. If he was chasing him, he would have shot him in the back. No…I think his companions dumped him here after shooting him to make sure he didn't say anything."

After talking with people at the marina and determining that no one had seen a tall English-looking man, they asked about the SUV. One older fisherman said he saw an SUV drive very fast past the marina just after dark.

Two army vehicles pulled up and told everyone to clear the area. Honey Boy and Mei Li left with the crowd. As they were walking away, a young boy approached them. "Do you look for your amigo, señor?"

"Yes. Have you seen anything?"

Unabashedly the boy stuck out his hand expecting to be paid for any information he might have. Honey Boy reached into his pocket, took out a ten dollar bill, and handed it to the boy.

Mei Li commented, "They start young, don't they?"

The boy looked at the money and told Honey Boy, "Last night, right after some people stopped their car and shot the man, a tall man came running up the street. He stopped and checked the man who was shot, then went across the street and stole a car."

"Stole a car? Why do you say that?"

"Because he broke a window, then used the wires to make it start."

"What kind of car was it?"

"A big car like the other one. A GMC, I think."

"Which way did he go?"

"That way," he said, pointing north.

"Is that the same direction the big car went?"

"Si, señor."

Which way is the airport?"

"It is the other way," said the boy, again pointing to emphasize his answer. "Where do you come from, señor?"

"Why do you want to know?"

"You are the second giant I see this week. The other man was like you, only bigger."

"That must have been Tyler," Mei Li said. "Where did you see him?"

"At Koko Chang's. He was eating a big bowl of fruit."

Honey Boy told the boy, "I'm from Hawaii. The other man is my brother. We are both looking for our friend. Here's another ten. Thank you for telling us what you know."

"Gracias, señor. Adios."

SEVENTY ONE

"There's something wrong with this whole picture, Mei Li," Honey Boy exclaimed as he got into the car.

"Why do you say that?"

"Think about it. There is no easy way off the Baja Peninsula except by plane, and even that is limited. Why would they head in the opposite direction of the airport? Who in the hell would try to escape on a slow ferry to Mexico?"

"Maybe they have a hidden airstrip and plane somewhere. Melvin said they had a large drug supply and millions in cash. They obviously didn't expect a raid, so they may be scrambling."

"If so, that will give Markham a little more time to find them and give us time to find him. Let me see that photo of Markham again."

Mei Li selected the photo on her phone and handed it to Honey Boy. "Doesn't look like a spy, does he?"

"Neither do you. Besides, what are spies supposed to look like?"

"Like the ones in movies, I guess. But you're right. Since neither of us look like spies, and we've never seen one another before, how is Markham going to know who we are and that we are on his side?"

"I thought our job is to find out if he is still alive and let Melvin know."

"It is. And if you want to call it quits, we can call Melvin right now and tell him we found people who saw someone that fits Markham's description."

"Not until we actually have eyes on him, and we're sure he doesn't need our help."

"So we're agreed?"

"Right."

"What's with all the flashing lights up ahead?"

"I don't know. How far are we from Santa Rosalia?"

"Ten to fifteen minutes. We should be able to see it pretty soon. According to the map we are approaching something called 'Puesto Control Militar.' Do you know what that is?"

"Nope. But it sounds like a military

post or something."

Honey Boy slowed the car as they approached what looked like an American port-of-entry. The road was channeled into turnoff lanes with soldiers directing traffic.

"Where is your pistol?"

"Under my jacket. Should I try to hide it?"

"No. We're close enough for them to see us. This could get dicey. Whatever happens, just be super polite and do whatever they tell us."

As they approached the covered check station, a soldier stepped out, directing with his hand where he wanted them to stop. Another soldier motioned for Honey Boy to roll his window down. "May I please see your identification and vehicle registration?" he asked.

Honey Boy handed the soldier the documents and waited while he made a notation on a clipboard.

"You are tourists, si?"

"Yes sir."

"What is your destination?"

"Santa Rosalia."

"You are nearly there. It is but a few miles further."

Handing the papers back to Honey

Boy he said in an officiously stern voice, "It is good you are traveling in the daytime. It is much safer for you Americans. With that, the soldier waved them on.

Honey Boy turned to Mei Li with a relieved look on his face. "Didn't expect that. We were lucky."

"Let's go ahead and check out the ferry boat. If we don't pick up any leads, we can always return to Loreto."

"How are we going to explain that, if we have to go through the check station again?"

"I'll think of something."

SEVENTY TWO

FBI Agent Davis, the U.S. Attorney General and the Director of the DEA from Washington, sat in front of Harry's desk carefully listening to him present all of the data regarding Tommy Thompson's money-laundering and real estate scheme. When the presentation was finished, the Attorney General said, "That is an amazing operation you just described. You realize this could seriously inhibit the drug trade for some time. Do you think El Jefe or Truong has any idea you know where their money is?"

"They know we're aware of some of their recent drug shipments. I've not seen anything indicating changes in the money operation. I really don't think they know what Tommy was up to."

Turning to Davis and the DEA director, the Attorney General said, "Mobilize a task force immediately. Coordinate with this Major Sandoval so we can hit all the banks at the same time."

Turning back to Harry, he said, "Thank you, Mr. Walters. You've done an outstanding job. Your government is grateful."

"How grateful?"

"Don't worry, Mr. Walters. I'm sure our appreciation will be commensurate with the magnitude of the recovery."

SEVENTY THREE

Honey Boy and Mei Li asked people at the ferry terminal if they had seen anyone fitting Markham's description. No one had seen a tall gringo, and no one with the name of Markham had purchased a ticket. (A bit of inside information ascertained by Mei Li's judicious use of twenty dollar bills.)

"When I was talking with the ticket agent," Mei Li explained, "she said she hadn't seen any English or American men last night. She asked if I was Chinese. When I said yes, she said there were two Chinese men here last night. They didn't take the ferry. They were here with an SUV that the ferry transported to the mainland. She said the two Chinese left with two other men, one who was a fair-skinned Mexican."

Mei Li called Melvin on their drive

back to Loreto to report what they had discovered so far. Then she asked, "Have you been able to reach Markham by phone yet?"

"Not a word. If you haven't made contact by the end of the day, I'll have you and Honey Boy report to Major Sandoval, and we'll come down and join you. Go back to the hotel and scope out the drug headquarters, then give me a call. The army and Federales will probably have that place under wraps for a long time.

"I have some military friends keeping track of any planes leaving the Baja area, so that leaves cars and boats as a way out. Do another check of any medical facilities there in Loreto; see if they treated Markham or any of Truong's crowd. Don't forget to check the pharmacies, as well, to see if they've sold any antibiotics or large quantities of bandages that might be used to treat gunshot wounds."

"Yes sir, boss. We're about five miles from Loreto. We'll start checking right away."

"That was a long, one-sided conversation. What did Melvin have to say?"

"He gave us specific orders to check the pharmacies and any medical facilities in Loreto to see if Markham may have been shot.

———————

About a half mile outside of Loreto, traffic slowed and came to a stop. Honey Boy and Mei Li found themselves in line at a military roadblock set up by Major Sandoval's men.

"Damn, this explains why the military check station was closed when we came back through."

"Looks like we're going to get searched. Call Melvin. Ask him if we should let these people know who we are, or just ditch the pistols."

Back on the phone, Melvin responded to Mei Li's question, "Keep the weapons concealed on your bodies and just act like tourists. If they frisk you and find the guns, I'll call Sandoval and clear everything. It'll be better if Sandoval doesn't think I'm working behind his back."

Mei Li shared Melvin's directive with Honey Boy, who said, "Give me your pistol."

"Why?"

"I'm big enough to hide it in my sock and I'll tuck mine in the back of my waistband. That way, if I'm found out, you won't be carrying."

"Still being big brother, huh?"

"Damn right. And it will be easier for you to call Melvin if you're not in cuffs."

"Okay, big braddah. Here you go. Be careful. It's loaded, you know."

Honey Boy slowly approached the barricade and stopped. On either side of the road were two, open personnel carriers with .50 caliber machine guns mounted on the back, pointing at their vehicle.

"This is no regular roadblock. Be very careful. These guys look serious," Honey Boy said to Mei Li.

One of the soldiers approached their vehicle and signaled for Honey Boy to roll down the window. When he did so, the soldier said, "Please park your vehicle over there. Someone will be there shortly to check your identification and registration. If you would please have both ready and stand at the rear of your vehicle, it will speed up the process."

"Yes, sir," Honey Boy replied. "What's this all about? I've never been stopped by the army before."

"Please park your vehicle as directed, sir," came the curt reply.

"Do you have your phone ready? We may not have much time. These guys are pros and it looks like they mean business."

Mei Li decided to call Melvin again while they were waiting. As she was explaining the situation to him, an officer and two soldiers with assault rifles came to them.

"Mr. Vili. Ms. Li. I'm Major Sandoval. Welcome to Mexico." Noting the stunned looks on their faces, he continued, "Don't be alarmed. We've been keeping track of you since your plane landed. I presume Colonel Momi sent you to find his friend?"

"Nice to meet you, Major. You are correct. We are here to determine what happened to Mr. Markham."

"Major Sandoval, Colonel Momi, as you know him, would like to talk with you." That said, Mei Li handed the phone to the major and waited until he hung up and handed her phone back to her.

"Please follow me. There is something you need to see."

Honey Boy and Mei Li looked at each other with worried glances. Mei Li asked Sandoval, "Is it Markham?"

"No, ma'am. It is, most likely, his handiwork, though."

Honey Boy and Mei Li got back in their car and followed the major to the house where El Jefe and Truong were the night before. Soldiers were posted all around the perimeter. People who appeared to be medical personnel were working in the yard and in the house.

"What happened?" Mei Li asked.

"So far, we have been able to determine that two men, one Mexican and one Chinese were killed here last night. Both of the men were stabbed. Their bodies were found outside the house. My medical team informed me that each man was killed by a knife through the back directly into the liver. That is a technique taught to commandos. The pain is so severe, it prevents a victim from yelling out. Does the man you are trying to find have this kind of skill?"

"Most likely. He is a former MI5 agent."

"I thought as much. It was easy to put two and two together and get four. Additionally, we have blood smear from someone who was sitting at the table. If the two cartel bosses were here, they are missing along with the man you're looking for.

"Colonel Momi and I agreed that it would be best for you to return home. I'm having two additional companies report to seal off Loreto and begin a door-to-door search. I'll have Sergeant Ruiz escort you to the airport. If you'll be kind enough to give the sergeant your weapons, I would appreciate it."

Honey Boy handed over the pistols. The major bid them goodbye. "Nice meeting you. Don't worry, we will find Colonel Momi's friend."

Mei Li replied, "Let's just hope he's alive when you do. Aloha, Major."

SEVENTY FOUR

The plane carrying Melvin and Kevin was once again met at the Loreto airport by Major Sandoval.

"Gentlemen, welcome back to Mexico."

"Thank you, Major. Any news?"

"Regrettably, no. It would seem that your man and the two drug lords have disappeared. Our sweep did result in finding a small meth lab and the arrest of two locals."

"As isolated as Loreto is, Major, you surely would have picked up on anyone leaving. Maybe they're still in town."

"My thoughts, as well, Colonel. Perhaps you will be able to get information from the citizens. No one is talking to us. They are all too afraid of repercussions from the cartels. Please keep me informed of your whereabouts, and if there is any shooting to be done, let us do it."

"If we have a choice, I'll be happy

279

to."

———————

After obtaining a vehicle, Melvin and Kevin drove to the house where the latest deaths occurred. They spent an hour or so gathering information and re-creating what happened.

Melvin said, "Sure looks like Markham's handiwork to me. Let's each take a different direction and check out the neighborhood. I presume they left on foot since the big SUV is still here. Take your time and keep your eyes open for anything that may give us a clue as to where they went from here. Let's meet back here in an hour."

Melvin took the street heading east. It was a sparsely-populated area with few occupied houses. He checked the two abandoned houses but didn't find anything.

Kevin checked the areas to the north and west. There were only three houses to the north, each occupied by families with children playing in the yard. "Not someplace you would want to hide," Kevin said to himself. To the west was a warren of buildings and houses, all leading to the center of Loreto.

Kevin then worked to the south, using his fluent Spanish to talk with several of the residents. They all claimed to have seen nothing. When the sun went down, they closed all the blinds and locked all the doors. Major Sandoval was correct. They were terrified of being caught in the middle.

As he headed back to rendezvous with Melvin, he spotted a dark spot on the sidewalk. He knelt down to examine the spot and concluded that it was blood. He continued on the walk for another ten feet or so, without finding any more blood, so he turned around and went in the opposite direction. This time, he found a larger drop and continued following drops that were about fifteen feet apart.

Kevin called Melvin, then waited until he joined him. Together they followed the trail, which was leading them toward the marina.

Melvin declared, "Whoever was leaking blood must not be too badly wounded. It looks like they were running, based on the distance between drops. Let's get a sample so we can see if it matches Forest's DNA."

The pair continued along their path until they reached the marina. There, they found the last blood drop at the end of a small side pier.

"Whoever we're following must have gotten on a boat, observed Kevin.

Melvin replied, "The question is who? And was there more than one?"

Melvin called Major Sandoval to meet them at the pier.

"Well, this explains why our sweep didn't turn up anything. They were out on the water."

"They?" asked Kevin.

"I assume they are all together. We would have found them if they were still in Loreto."

Noting the severity of Sandoval's pronouncement, Melvin said, "I agree. How can we check on the boats that were here?"

"The harbor master will have a record of the larger boats, but they don't pay much attention to all the small fishing boats. It saves the fishermen slip fees. We occasionally do random searches for drugs, but rarely find anything. The cartel generally uses big boats, because they're easier to smuggle drugs onto.

"I'll call in air support. We can do a fly-over of this area and search all along the coast. If you want to search the coast between here and the airport, I'll go back to my office and get things started."

"Thank you, Major."

"Does your friend know anything about boats?"

"Yes, he does. He's an expert sailor. He even owns his own boat."

"That won't make it any easier to find him."

"Probably not. See you soon, Major."

SEVENTY FIVE

Melvin sent Kevin to check along the coast, while he headed south toward the airport. No one along the mile-and-one-half route had seen or heard any boats, nor did they know of any strange men in the area. All were curious as to why the army had sealed off the town. They garnered more information from Melvin than he was able to get from them.

Kevin had the same result. The area north of the marina was less populated and the coastline even more undeveloped.

Regrouping at Major Sandoval's office, Melvin and the major were going over the air search plans.

"I see a couple of possibilities where a boat could hide, Colonel Momi. The big bay area of Puerto Escondido, and the two big islands, Coronado and Danzante."

"What is this little marina?"

"That's Loreto Shores. It's a nice RV park and resort owned by Americans. It caters to the motor home people, and to the sportsmen who come down here to fish the Sea of Cortez for dorado, or mahi as you call them. They have a boat rental and storage facility."

"We'll go look around there while you do your aerial surveillance."

"Good idea. It's just a few minutes away."

———————

Loreto Shores lived up to Major Sandoval's billing. There were several expensive motor homes and a few smaller RVs on the lot. The casas, or suites, had a number of upscale cars parked in front of them. Melvin, and Kevin walked over to a fish-cleaning station near the boat dock where three men were dispatching the day's catch.

"Nice mahi. Bigger than the ones I've caught recently in Hawaii," said Melvin.

"Best fishing in the world. I come

down here every year. Never been disappointed."

"What does it cost to rent a boat and some gear?"

"It would only be a couple hundred each. That's nothing for this kind of fishing."

"Who do we see about renting a boat?"

"That would be Billy. He's the homeless-looking guy over there by the boat storage area."

Melvin thanked the fisherman, then he and Kevin went to find Billy. On the way, they took careful note of their surroundings. As they neared the boat storage, they were greeted by a deep, gravelly voice. "You boys look lost. Can I help you?"

Melvin replied, "You may, if you're Billy."

"Indeed I am."

"Good. My name is Melvin Momi. I'm a private investigator from Hawaii. This is my associate, Kevin Whitehill. We're looking for a friend of ours who came down here to Loreto a few days ago. We haven't heard from him since." Showing Billy a photo of Markham, Melvin said, "Have you seen him, by any chance?"

"No. Those fishermen are the only

new folks to come in this past week. The others are all regulars. Your friend a fisherman?"

"Not so much. He is an avid sailor, though, and we thought he may have rented a boat from you."

"I had a boat stolen from the marina in Loreto. Or at least that's the story from the damn drunk I rented it to. He took the boat and a lady who has a motorhome here, into town to the marina. They spent the afternoon and a better part of the night drinking. I guess they got really soused, and decided to spend the night at La Mision. Next morning when he went to the boat, it wasn't there. I hope to hell I can find it. It's a 40-foot cabin cruiser, and one of my newer boats. Have you ever dealt with Mexican insurance companies? I may not live long enough to settle a claim."

"Thanks for your time. If our friend should show up here, would you call me at this number?" asked Melvin, handing him a business card.

"You bet. And if you happen to see my boat while you're looking for your friend, you can call me," replied Billy, as he handed Melvin one of his cards.

SEVENTY SIX

Sandoval and Melvin reviewed the results of their searches and still had few leads as to what may have happened to Markham, El Jefe and Truong.

Sandoval told Melvin and Kevin, "My units were successful in shutting down the distribution centers at Topolobampo, Santa Rosalia and Los Mochis. Next, we will be moving to La Paz and Cabo San Lucas. "We will continue to search for your friend. We are very interested in finding El Jefe and Truong and your Mr. Markham, as well. Providing they didn't cross over to mainland Mexico, we will eventually locate them. The Baja is like an island. As they say, 'you can run, but you can't hide.'"

In the midst of Sandoval's commentary, Melvin's cell rang. It was Harry. Melvin listened carefully for several minutes, then announced to Harry he had switched over to the speaker mode.

"Major Sandoval, my name is Harold Walters. I'm an attorney in San Diego. Mr. Momi, his staff, and I have been trying for over a year to trace the money trail of a Chinese and Mexican drug cartel operating in Hawaii, California and Mexico. Several federal agencies have formed a task force to seize some twenty-four banks we believe are holding drug funds. Four of those banks are in Mexico. If you would be agreeable to spearheading the seizure of the four Mexican banks, at the same time as we move on the American banks, I will have Melvin give you the details. Can we rely on your assistance?"

"Why me? Shouldn't you be working through the Mexican federal police?"

"It's a matter of trust. This needs to happen very soon, and Melvin assures me you are trustworthy. We may lose the element of surprise, and a lot of money, if we have to take time to vet out another person in Mexico."

"What you say is true. But I would be crossing a lot of political lines. How much money are you talking about?"

In Mexico, nearly seven hundred fifty million dollars and over two and a-half billion dollars in the United States."

"Are you licensed to practice in

Mexico, Mr. Walters?"

"As a matter of fact, I am. Why?"

"I'll need a good attorney if I get arrested when this is all over."

"I think any problems will disappear if you turn over several billion pesos to the politicians."

"I would agree. You have my cooperation."

Harry directed Melvin to give Sandoval the names, account information, and locations of the four Mexican banks, along with the contact number for FBI Agent Davis.

SEVENTY SEVEN

Melvin and Kevin returned to the marina where they found several fishermen they hadn't talked to earlier. Kevin greeted one of the men in Spanish and was pleased to learn he had seen Markham yesterday at the marina.

"Did he have anyone with him?"

"Si, señor. He had two prisoners."

"Two prisoners? Why do you think they were prisoners?"

"They had their hands tied behind them, and he was a soldier with a military rifle. I presumed they were prisoners"

"A military rifle?"

"Si, señor. It was an automatic, like you see the soldiers using when they show them on television."

"Were any of the men injured?"

"One of the prisoners had a cut and a large bruise on his forehead. The soldier had a bloody arm."

"What did the prisoners look like?"

"One was an older Asian man about my size. The other was about six feet tall and younger. He may have been Americano. He was the one with the injured face."

"Did you see where they went?"

"The soldier put them on a new boat and sailed out of the marina toward La Paz.

"Do you have any idea why he would sail toward La Paz? Is there an army base there?"

"No, señor. The army base is the other way, near Santa Rosalia. There is a federal police station in La Paz. Maybe he was taking the prisoners there."

"Do the soldiers usually use boats to transport prisoners?"

"Sometimes. Boats are less noticeable than the prison buses. This new boat they have looks like all the tourist fishing boats."

"Thank you, my friend."

As Melvin and Kevin walked back to their vehicle, Melvin said, "Well that confirms Markham was alive when he got on the boat."

"And that he may have had Truong and El Jefe with him. Where do you think he would have taken them?"

"Let's go over our map again. Major

Sandoval has done a pretty thorough search. Let's see if we can spot an area he might have missed."

The pair spent the next fifteen minutes carefully going over every square inch of the map hoping to find some clue as to Markham's whereabouts. Getting nothing, Melvin called Major Sandoval to ask about the aerial surveillance he had performed. "We talked with someone at the marina who confirmed that Markham was using the boat we thought. Did you see any boats similar to it in your search?"

"My pilot spotted three boats of that size. He said they were all fishing boats."

"He was sure they were fishing boats?"

"I asked him the same question. He said they were all near the good dorado runs between Loreto and Isla Carmen. All three boats were catching fish. Do you want me to have him do another search?"

"I would really appreciate that. Would it be possible for Kevin and me to go with him?"

"Certainly. I'll make the call. You can meet the pilot at the airport.

The view from the cockpit of the small plane gave Melvin several miles of clear visibility. Kevin was seated just behind the cockpit and could observe the boat traffic below from either side of the plane.

As they neared Isla Carmen, the pilot saw a boat and flew towards it. Melvin and Kevin zeroed in on the vessel with the high-powered military binoculars the pilot gave them. They could clearly see the four Mexican fishermen plying their trade. Several boats later, there was still no sign of Markham.

The pilot made a full-circle sweep of Isla Carmen and the two main coves where a boat could moor. He then headed toward La Paz and the shoreline back to Loreto.

"There!" Melvin cried, pointing to a spot on the right. "That looks like a new boat." As the plane approached the vessel, both Kevin and Melvin confirmed it was the boat they were searching for. "Kevin, do you see any sign of Markham?"

"No. I see footprints in the sand leading up to some shrubbery where the boat is tied off."

The pilot banked the plane to circle the boat. Melvin and Kevin took note of its location and logged the GPS coordinates into their cell phones. The boat was tied up on a small sprit of sand about a quarter mile from Loreto Shores RV Park. There were two older buildings nearby with a dirt road leading to the main road.

"Get us back to the airport so we can check this out on the ground," Melvin excitedly ordered the pilot.

SEVENTY EIGHT

The buildings Melvin and Kevin had spotted from the airplane were easy to find. The GPS coordinates confirmed it was the right place. Nearing the buildings, Kevin told Melvin, "Let's ease up to that building on the right. It looks more accessible than the other one."

"I agree. Be ready in case someone opens fire on us."

Melvin parked on the west side of the ramshackle structure. Both men exited the vehicle and checked their weapons before moving forward. Melvin motioned for Kevin to go around the building on the right and he went left. All of the windows had been boarded, so there was no way of seeing inside. Both men listened for any noise. Hearing none, they proceeded to the front of the building where there was a door.

With weapons at the ready, Melvin slowly turned the knob and opened the door.

Gazing into the darkened interior, they saw an object in the center of the room. When their eyes grew accustomed to the darkness, they saw two men tied to a bench. The men neither moved nor made any sound. When Kevin and Melvin got close enough to see the men's faces, they could see that they were unconscious.

"This is El Jefe and Truong," Kevin said in disbelief. "I wonder what happened to Forest!"

"I'm right here," came a quiet voice out of the dark recess of a corner. "Are you by yourselves? Or did you bring the Mexican army with you?"

"Just us, Forest," Melvin responded. "Are you okay?"

"I've a nick or two from the shootout and a tussle with the bodyguards, but nothing that won't heal." Switching on a small lamp he had brought from the boat, Markham illuminated the room. Looking down at the two men on the bench with their heads slumped down, Markham said, "I'd like for you to meet Sergei Obelensky and Wa Tak Truong."

"Obelensky. That's Russian, isn't it? Who is he?" asked Kevin.

"He's El Jefe. It seems he killed

Ochoa and took over the cartel."

Melvin asked, "What's wrong with them?" Did you drug them or something?"

"I gave them each a little love tap when I heard you approaching. They'll come around in a little while."

"I hope so. We've got a lot of questions."

"They've been pretty talkative so far, but there's more to learn, I'm sure."

"I'll be happy to kill them both!" blurted Kevin.

Markham placed a hand on his shoulder. "That would make us animals as low as they. We'll need to get them out of Mexico, however. They would be out of a Mexican prison faster than they went in."

"I agree," said Melvin. "Perhaps Major Sandoval could assist."

"I don't think we should take the chance," responded Kevin.

"I still have the boat I borrowed. It would be a little tricky, but I think I could get it all the way to California."

"You might not have to take it to California if I can get Commander Dawson to meet us in open water," said Melvin.

Truong was the first to awaken. He blinked his eyes several times and showed a bit of surprise when he found himself staring at the face of Melvin Momi. "Mr. Momi. At last we meet. You have been a most worthy adversary."

"Cut the inscrutable act. You can't spend enough time in hell to make up for all the lives you're responsible for destroying…especially my wife's!"

Obelensky lolled his head back and forth a couple of times, then raised it, and opened his eyes. Several moments passed until he was coherent enough to realize that two new people were in the room. Looking at Markham, he asked, "Who are your friends?"

"Melvin Momi and Kevin Whitehill."

"Whitehill? I know that name. You're Arona, from Tijuana. Damned undercover American cop."

"One and the same." Kevin stood menacingly over him and asked, "Why did you have my wife killed? What did you do with her body?"

"No reason not to tell you. When I found out you were a DEA pig, I sent Ramon and Estaban to kidnap your wife. I was going to use her as leverage to get you to tell us everything you knew about our business. She went all cop and shot Estaban. He went nuts and choked her to death."

"What did you do with her body?"

"She was cremated. We have a small mortuary and crematorium in Chula Vista that we use from time-to-time to get rid of evidence."

Kevin shuddered and began weeping uncontrollably. Melvin moved him away and softly said, "At least now you know."

Turning around, Melvin heard Markham ask, "How long has "The Wolf" been dead?"

"Ochoa? A couple of years, now. He was too dumb to run a cartel. He thought I was his best friend right up until I put a bullet in his forehead."

"Did you know he kidnapped and killed my wife after I busted his setup in Matzatlán?"

"He didn't do it. I did. I was going to have you killed, too, but he wouldn't let me. I told you he was dumb."

"Are you trying to get us both killed?" screamed Truong. "Shut your mouth! You're the foolish one."

"Foolish one? Do you think they would ever turn us over to the Federales? This one knows the minute I get a phone in my hand, I'll have them all killed."

Kevin, in a blind rage, unbuckled and

removed his belt, walked behind El Jefe, and placed the belt around his neck. "You're going to see what it's like to slowly quit breathing."

"Wait! Forest commanded. "That's too easy. I think he needs a taste of his own medicine." He walked over to one of the cases brought from the boat and opened it. He withdrew a sack of cocaine and brought it over to El Jefe. Cutting into the package, he put some of the powder on the knife blade and held it under El Jefe's nose. Then he forced him to inhale the powder. After repeating the process several times, El Jefe was a wild man. He was squirming and trying to get off the bench. Markham began asking him questions about location, supply routes, and financing of the cartel. With each repeated dose of cocaine, El Jefe revealed more and more information. Then he began to spasm and became unresponsive. "Okay, Kevin. He's all yours." A few minutes later, El Jefe sat lifeless. Kevin put his belt back on and walked outside.

"He just crossed a line he can never come back from. Why don't you go outside, Melvin, and see if he's all right? I can take care of business in here."

"We really don't have a choice, do

we?"

"No, but you do. Go outside and let me take care of this."

SEVENTY NINE

Seated around a large conference table in Harry's office were the Attorney General, Agent Davis of the FBI, the DEA director, Tyler, and Harry.

After introductions were made, the Attorney General addressed the group. "Gentlemen, I want to thank you all for your help in shutting down one of the largest known drug operations in Hawaii, California and Mexico. Speaking of Mexico, I've been informed by my counterpart that Major Sandoval is being promoted to General, and will be heading a new anti-drug division funded by some of the money recovered from the Mexican banks.

"On our side of the border, we seized $2.63 billion and arrested thirty-four people for money-laundering and numerous other crimes. That will keep them out of circulation for quite a few years.

"True to my promise, Mr. Walters, I

am happy to inform you that the Government Accounting Office will be bringing you a tax-free, ten percent, finder's fee sometime next week.

"You have my sincerest thanks and, Mr. Walters, would you please extend our thanks to General Sandoval? I understand you are still working with him on the search for Mr. Markham and the two drug kingpins."

"Yes, sir. I'll give him your message."

Shortly after the Attorney General and his entourage departed, Sandoval came into the office and was ushered into the conference room by Sunny.

Tyler stood and snapped a smart salute. "General, welcome. To what do we owe the honor of your visit? Do you have any news on Markham?"

"Thank you. The only news I have that may relate to Mr. Markham is this," said Sandoval, as he handed Tyler an article clipped from the Ensenada La Mexicana newspaper.

Tyler looked at the article and accompanying photograph, then handed it to Harry.

"Since your Spanish is better than mine, Tyler, Would you like to translate this?"

Tyler scanned the article and blurted out, "They got the sons-a-bitches!"

Glancing up at the inquisitive faces, he began to read. "Dateline yesterday from Loreto.

Early-morning visitors to the Mission of Our Lady of Loreto, the first of eighteen mission churches in Baja California founded by the Jesuits in 1697, were horrified to see two men hanging from a cross in the courtyard.

A handwritten sign was nailed to the center of the cross. It read: VENGEANCE IS MINE. Below the cross was a large pile of white powder. The federal police have identified it as cocaine, with an estimated street-value of over ten million pesos. The police also found a briefcase on the altar in the mission,

305

that held over one million American dollars.

The two dead men have been identified as Wa Tak Truong of China and Sergei Obelensky, a Russo-Mexican, also known as El Jefe, the suspected leader of one of the largest drug cartels in Mexico. Truong was a suspected narcotrafficker in Hawaii and California.

The police said no one has come forward to claim credit for the deaths. They will continue their investigation, but at this time, have no further information.

See related story, **DRUG MONEY SEIZED,** on page six.

Tyler stopped and looked at the other news article stapled to the first one, then continued, "This is concerning the raid on the Mexican banks, headed by General Sandoval, and what the Attorney General told us about his promotion."

"Perhaps we will be able to work together again." General Sandoval said, looking at Harry. If Mr. Markham returns, would you please give him my thanks? His actions obviously resulted in our being able to disband the cartel."

Tyler chuckled out loud. As everyone turned to see what he thought was so funny, he pointed to the conference room door and said, "Why don't you tell him yourself?"

Standing in the doorway, in a Mexican army uniform, was a bandaged and bedraggled Markham. Following closely behind were Kevin and Melvin.

Sandoval studied the man in front of him for a few moments, then extended his hand, "Boat shoes are not standard army issue, Corporal. Should I ask how you came about the uniform?"

"Let us just say, the gentleman who previously wore it was fond of my cowboy boots."

"Mr. Markham, my personal thanks and the thanks of Mexico for ridding us of El Jefe and Truong."

Tyler handed Forest the newspaper clippings. Markham carefully read the article and told Sandoval, "I don't know why you think I had anything to do with this. It seems someone exhibited a great deal of wrath toward these two gents."

Sandoval responded with, "As far as the people of Mexico and I are concerned, it is just the right amount of wrath."

EPILOGUE

At his vacation home on Molokai, Harry sat on his lanai sipping a chilled glass of Prosecco and enjoying the company of his cohorts. Harry thought it quite appropriate to celebrate the conclusion of the Truong case where it had started.

As the sun began to set and the trade winds calmed for the evening, Harry addressed his colleagues with a toast. "Aloha, 'ohana. Nō ka 'oi. Kevin, since you're new, I just said, 'Hello, family. You're the best.' Welcome to the family. Now I understand Honey Boy has something to say."

Honey Boy stood, and blushing like a young boy declared, "Patty and I are getting married. We would like for you all to be at the wedding."

When the big round of applause and congratulations subsided, Harry continued, "If it's all right with all of you, I would like to give them their wedding present now."

After nods of approval, Harry handed Honey Boy a cashiers' check for five hundred thousand dollars. "Thanks for your help."

Patty looked at the check, jumped up, and grasped Harry in a bear hug, lifting him up off the floor. She gave him a big kiss on the cheek. "You the best boss evah, haole."

"That's part of the two hundred sixty million dollar finder's fee. I would also like to set up a scholarship fund for Manuel Ortega, in thanks for providing our last clue to the money."

He walked around the lanai, handing envelopes to Kevin, Tyler, Melvin and Markham. The contents of the envelopes listed details on account codes and security procedures to access fifty million dollars each as their share of the finder's fee. Next, he gave Mei Li a cashier's check for five hundred thousand dollars, saying, "That's for protecting Honey Boy."

Tyler picked Mei Li up with one arm, "We're going to Tonga and raise kids."

Kevin said, "I am going to take Sharon's mother and move to the Gulf Coast."

Markham said, "I'm going to refit my *Angel of Mercy* and sail her down to Bora Bora."

Melvin said, "I'm staying on Oahu. With this money, I can open a homeless shelter over by Makaha. That is, if Honey Boy will take over the agency for me."

Then they all turned to Harry to hear his plan. "Well, I think I'm going to semi-retire."

"Semi-retire?" asked Dayna.

"I'll probably sell the San Diego office to my partners, and just keep the Molokai office open. That all depends if I can find a new secretary to replace Patty." Turning to Dayna, he asked, "Would you like to be my new secretary?"

"You big nut, Harry! How am I going to be your secretary? I would have to move to Molokai, and that sounds like a low-paying, part-time job to me."

"Well, your full-time job could be here as well, with me, as Mrs. Harry Walters again. It doesn't pay anything, but it has unlimited benefits."

"If you really retire, I'll accept that job.

OTHER TITLES BY GARY CARR

• Just the Right Amount of Wrong

Attorney Harry Walters just wants to get away from the hustle and bustle of his busy San Diego law firm. For him, the Island of Molokai in Hawaii is a perfect paradise where he can handle simple cases and still feel like he's on vacation. Just when he thinks he can relax, the tranquility of paradise is disturbed when a family re8uyion turns deadly. When he reluctantly agrees to represent one of the family members, the case plunges him into a world of deceit, drugs, corruption and death. Harry and his investigative team follow a dangerous and unpredictable path to its explosive conclusion. Will he survive when the truth is uncovered?

• Just the Right Amount of Regret

Attorney Harry Walters made the trip from San Diego to Santa Barbara with mixed feelings. His ex-partner was dead–murdered. As troubling as it was to do the right thing and attend the funeral, the probability of running into his ex-wife was even worse. Harry was still bitter. He consoles himself by believing he can just quietly slip in and then out of town. But when his old partner's wife pleads for his help, he can't refuse and decides to stay. Harry has barely started to unravel the strange mystery when he is confronted by a bullet, his deepest emotions and a web of secrets, lies and corruption. Harry and his team of investigators must navigate a deadly maze before he can return home to San Diego–assuming he survives.

ABOUT THE AUTHOR

Gary calls himself a "Jack-of-All-Trades" and master of five. His curiosity and drive have led him to become a radio announcer, newspaper and television journalist, chef and restauranteur, building contractor and school administrator. Now that he is retired, he and his wife travel extensively, and delight in experiencing the many cultures the world has to offer. His love of food and people are reflected in his writing.